Sands of Passion

D1525485

Published by Phaze Books
Also by Dahlia Rose

The Collettes Trilogy
(print collection)

Also available as separate eBooks:

The Collettes: Sola
The Collettes: Luna
The Collettes: Willa

Cincinnati, Ohio

www.Phaze.com

Sands of Passion

two novellas of erotic romance by

DAHLIA ROSE

PHAZE
Cincinnati, Ohio

A Phaze Production
Phaze Books
6470A Glenway Avenue, #109
Cincinnati, OH 45211-5222
Phaze is an imprint of Mundania Press, LLC.

To order additional copies of this book, contact:
books@phaze.com
www.Phaze.com

Cover art © 2008 Debi Lewis
Edited by Pat Sager and Stacia Seaman

Trade Paperback ISBN-13: 978-1-60659-068-3

First Print Edition – October, 2008
Printed in the United States of America

10 9 8 7 6 5 4 3 2 1

Caribbean Blue

Chapter One

The sky was a deep blue, one of the deepest blues he had ever seen. Gem Air landed and taxied down the small Runway at Grantley Adams International Airport in Barbados. The smiling face of the stewardess ushered the passengers off the steel bird and each of them stepped out into the sunlight. Elijah Connors was one of those passengers and when he stepped into the clean, bright sunshine of the island he put his sunglasses on against the glare. He thought better of it and took them off once again. He didn't want the darkness of the lenses to spoil the beauty of the island. He looked around as he walked across the tarmac to the central building of the airport. The palm trees waved in the cool breeze and the exotic smells of the isle filled his nostrils.

Yeah, I made a good decision to visit here, he thought as he entered into the customs line. He was thirty-five with dark brown hair and eyes just as dark. Being a cop in Philadelphia was tough and he was burning out. And old friend who relocated to Barbados encouraged him to come down for a vacation and Eli decided to take him up on the offer.

He went through the mandatory procedures of the island pretty quick and soon he was stepping into the sunshine once again. Even though he was inland he heard the waves crashing against the beach. Looking around he caught sight of his long time friend and his host for the next two weeks. A grin broke out on his face while he crossed the street.

"Hey, guy! So now I see why you left Philly!" Eli said. He grabbed his friend hand then on impulse embraced him in a hug. He hadn't seen Mick since he retired from the police force and moved here to marry his sweetheart.

"Well, Eli, you are as pale as ever. Philly in November must be cold as shit." Mick grinned and slapped Eli's back. "Come on get in the car and let's go to the house."

"Where is this house anyway?"

"You'll see buddy, you'll see."

Mick's house turned out to be right on the cliffs in St Lucy parish. They were steps cut out of the limestone that led down to the white sandy beach. Waves with foamy caps lapped at the sand and the water was the bluest Eli had ever seen.

"Now this is a house, Mick! Wanna adopt me?"

Mick laughed. "The wife won't let me."

As they walked up the gravel walkway a woman with dark bronze skin walked out to greet them. She wrapped her arms around Mick's waist and kissed him full on the lips.

"You got your friend safely then?" Her accent was thick and distinctly of the islands.

"Sure his plane landed on time, babe," Mick replied with a smile. "This is Elijah Connors. Eli, this is my wife, Jewel."

Eli could see the love in his eyes for his new wife and felt a pang of something deep inside himself. "Very nice to meet you, Jewel. I love your home and Mick won't adopt me."

She laughed in turn. "Maybe after we have a few of our own you can be our next child. Or maybe you will like the island so much you won't leave. Stranger things have happened."

"It's a nice thought, but I have work in Philly and I only have a two-week vacation."

"Hmmmm, we shall see," Jewel. The hint of mystery that made Eli curious. Come on inside and have some mango juice. I made lunch. Then you can go explore if you like or rest in your room."

"Thank God it's lunch time!" Mick said rubbing his hands together while the three of them walked in to the house.

"I can see you still love your stomach," Eli joked.

Lunch turned out to be fried fish and big thick potatoes wedges. Maybe it was the weather or the fresh air but Eli ate the delicious food like he had been starving for weeks. Even Mick's teasing at his expense did not deter him. He went up to the room Jewel had made up for him. A bed with a wispy mosquito netting stood in the middle of a perfectly white room with whicker furniture that complemented the island décor. He opened the French doors that led outside to the cliff and the steps leading down to the beach. Walking back over to the bed, he lay down and looked out to the horizon and felt his entire body relax. He needed this more than he thought. Outside the doors the sea made a lulling sound blended with the sounds of tropical birds calling out to each other and the breeze going through the lush vegetation of the island. Another sound mixed in with the island's own brand of music.

What is that singing? Eli passed it of as his imagination until he heard it again and this time laughter accompanied it. He sat up from his position across the bed and looked towards the open doors. He heard the tinkling laughter again, it was like water babbling across rocks and he smiled at the infectious sound. Eli was curious to see who it came from so he stepped out onto the verandah and looked down to the beach. He saw no one on the sand but yet the laughter and another line of what he assumed was an island song came to his ears.

I have to know where that is coming from. He thought and stepped out from the verandah on to the stepped that led down to the beach. Each step brought the melody louder to his ears and it began to captivate his senses. He was reminded of the Greek myths where men's ships were led onto the rocks by the sensual Siren's songs. He stepped around the rocks that made the wall of the cliff to the other side of the beach. Still no one came into sight. Where was the singer who charmed him with her tempting song? He walked further down the sand and found another set of rocks. He let his fingers trail around the damp stone as he walked, the surf came up and washed around his feet. The water was warm and that alone made him want to take a swim. But not now, he was so close to discovering where the voice was coming from.

There she was. Eli stared at the beauty in front of him and his breath caught in his throat. Her hair was long tight curls of black flowing down to her waist. Her skin glowed from being kissed by the sun but her eyes were only a few shades darker than the sand at their feet. Around her neck was the smooth body of a snake and she held its flat head in her hands. She sang a few lines of the same song to her pet, waiting silently as if she was listening to the snake talk, before laughing out loud. Throwing her head back and letting the sound flow from her. He had never seen anything so unrestrained and free.

"Hi there. I like your song. What is it called?" Eli asked.

She swirled around to face him and it was then he saw the full beauty of her oval face, the side view did not do her justice. He walked slowly over to her because her green eyes were filled with wariness. She began to leave, but somehow Eli didn't want her to.

"Hey, hey, don't go! I won't hurt you. I just heard you singing that's all." His voice gentled, hoping she would not be afraid to stay.

"I was singing to Columbus."

Eli wanted to roll his eyes in pleasure as her voice was over him like the waves on her bare feet. "Columbus is your pet?" referring to the nine-foot yellow boa she had around her neck.

"We take care of each other. He is not my pet."

"What were you singing to him?"

"A song I was taught as a child. It's about mermaids that come on land to play with mortals and make hibiscus crowns." She looked around as if she heard something that Eli could not hear. "I have to go now, goodbye."

"Hey, wait! Don't go!" he called after her. He followed her as she dashed off between the rocks and trees and was out of sight before he knew it. Eli still went after her the urge to follow her was fat too great to resist.

He heard her tinkling laughter from behind a tree and he looked behind it she ran behind the large trunk of a tree laden with fruit. A grin broke out on his face at his new game. Each time he looked around another tree she was already gone and peeking from the one right next to it.

"So what is this game we are playing?" Eli asked.

"Who says we are playing a game? I go, you follow. I cannot seem to lose you," she said with merriment dancing in her eyes.

He moved again and she twisted quickly, evading his and as it barely missed her arm. "What's your name, island girl?"

"And why should I tell you?"

Shoot, just missed her! He leaned against the tree trunk and laughed softly. He was having too much fun playing with this unknown woman. He felt like a teenage boy again.

"Tired?" Her head came around right above his shoulder and Eli was staring into her beautiful eyes.

"I'm an old man, I can't go running through the jungle chasing a strange woman," he replied.

"I left, you followed, so where is the chase? You aged rather well, old man. How old are you anyway. since you call yourself old.

"I'm thirty-five, so I have to be much older than you, I'd say you are about eighteen."

"You flatter me with the compliment, but I am closer to thirty, twenty eight to be exact."

"Are you going to tell me your name, island girl?" Eli cajoled softly. Sitting on the ground having a conversation with this woman was one of the best dialogues he ever had.

"Questions, questions. I'll tell you next time...maybe," she replied. She touched him on the nose with one finger before she scrambled up and ran off.

Eli watched her go with a huge grin spread across his face. She was amazing, moving as if her feet never touched the ground. Eli didn't know who she was but he swore he had just met one of the mermaids she was singing about coming to play on the island.

Chapter Two

Two days later, Eli was still thinking about the girl he met on the beach. Sitting across from Mick and his wife for breakfast, he pushed his eggs around on the plate.

"Homesick already?" Mick commented after watching him for a few minutes.

"What? Oh no, not at all!" Eli replied. "I'm loving it here."

On that point he was telling the truth. In the two days since he landed on the island he had spent most of his time at the beach, on jet skis, or a Catamaran out in the crystal blue water. Mick had given him a fishing pole and in the evenings he sat on the jetty with his legs hung over the edge. His fishing line was in the water but he didn't care if he caught a thing. Watching the sun set where it looked like the ocean met the sky was breathtaking. He slept like a rock each night. The only thing was he could not get the girl out of his mind. He looked for her over and over again but since the day he saw her she never came back.

"Have you guys ever seen a girl with dark long hair along this beach? She has a snake with her." Eli asked the question, looking at Mick and his wife.

"No, never seen her," Mick said with a shrug and went back to his food. But he caught a look in Jewel's eyes before she could cast them back down to her plate.

"What about you, Jewel, ever seen her?" Eli's cop instinct kicked in when he saw the look in her eye. She knew something.

"I have never seen such a girl on this beach, Eli." Jewel answered. "But the way you described her reminds me of a legend on the island."

"Here we go, another legend of the island," Mick teased and was rewarded with a slap on the back of his head by his wife.

Eli grinned knowing that if anyone had tried that with Mick when he was a cop in Philly they would be picking up their teeth from the floor. His friend had mellowed out since his move to the blissful peace of the island. "What is the legend about, Jewel?"

She sat forward with her fingers entwined under her chin and her tone took on a hint of mystery like a true storyteller. "It is said here on the island lives a small tribe of people named the Baqeu. They live in the hidden caves and gullies around the island and have found it easy to move around without being seen. Their leader is a witch doctor who had given them all the gift of magic. These women could not have children and because of this they wait until a family sleeps at night and puts the whole household under a spell. They steal babies from the family and take them to where they live to raise them as their own. The children are never seen again."

"What else?" Eli felt himself being drawn into the story and waited in anticipation for Jewel to finish her tale.

"There was one family that came here for a vacation. They were one from the island and moved to New York. They visited the island regularly so their children would not forget where they came from. This visit they had a new baby, a little girl who had hair like a crow's wing and eyes just as dark. Somehow the leader of the tribe saw her and wanted her for his own daughter. He watched her night and day until one night he put the family under a spell in their guesthouse and stole the baby away. The next morning the whole family searched the island, the police and so many who wanted to help they lost count of volunteers who searched for the child. They said a storm came in and you could hear her mother screaming her name over the howling of the wind. But they never found her and the family left the island months later broken hearted at losing their child and vowed never to return. That was twenty-two years ago, and to this day some say they see a young woman with dark eyes and a snake around her neck roaming the island as she pleases. Who ever tries to talk with her, she runs away and the island helps her hide."

At the end of her story Jewel sat back in her chair. Eli could see she believed every word of what the fable but of course he saw it as only an old wives' tale. Somehow something in the story made the hair in the back of his neck stand on end and gave him goose bumps along his arms. Was that the girl he saw on the beach? It was too much of a coincidence.

"Can't she weave a great yarn? I swear I should take her to Philly and put her in O'Malley's to tell her stories." Mick took up Jewels hand and kissed it softly.

In return she swatted him affectionately. "Be gone with you both. I have to clean up and get to the hospital for work."

As she walked over to the sink Eli had to ask one more question. "Jewel, what was the name of the baby that was stolen?

Jewel looked at him with quiet eyes. "Yes, I could never forget that name from the time I heard it growing up. Her name was Alison." She went back to cleaning up the dishes.

Eli got up and kissed her on the cheek and thanked her for breakfast. He went back upstairs and lay across the bed looking out to the ocean. His thoughts ran in circles from the story to the girl he saw. Could she have been his imagination? He wouldn't know unless he saw her again, *if* he ever saw her again.

* * * *

It was early evening before he got to be alone for a walk on the beach. When Mick had moved he had become head of security for one of the biggest hotel casinos on the island. So while Jewel was off at her job as a nurse at the local hospital, Eli went to the hotel with Mick who he could tell was trying to steer him into taking a job there. As he walked, Eli had to admit the idea of staying on the island had become more and more pleasant in only two days. He could see himself working in the various hotel chains and coming home to a balcony that overlooked the water. Listening to Calypso as it floated across the water from the various party boats bobbing on the waves. That was what Mick had offered him a suite in the hotel to live in just as long as he became his second in command. He'd known Mick inviting him down to Barbados had an ulterior motive behind it. As far as ulterior motives went, it was not a bad one.

The sun was just beginning to set as Eli walked and when he looked back he saw that he walked further then he had expected to go. *That's what you get for letting your mind wander.* He didn't mind too much as he turned to walk back. His gaze caught a flash of something moving in the clump of trees further up the sand. He thought is was a trick of light until he saw the flash of blue that was out of place in between the lush green trees. Following his instinct to always investigate he walked cautiously up to the grove. Eli stepped in between the low hanging branches and the flower filled vines, which hung all around. He saw it again and this time the black hair that went with it and his heart leapt with excitement. *It's her!*

"Hey, come back!" he called racing after the girl that moved quickly through the soft grass that grew over the sand. All he got in response was the tinkling giggle as he moved further into the grove. It seemed every leaf, branch or vine wanted to get in his way or slap at him as he tried to reach her. But he was not going to be deterred. Eli kept moving even though the further he went the vegetation got thicker. He finally came to a clearing where wild flowers grew in vibrant colors. He looked around at the fruit laden trees as all their different exotic scents assaulted his senses. In his whole life Eli could say he had never seen such beauty nestled in one place. When the girl stepped out into the clearing from the other side of the trees, he felt the splendor around him pale in comparison to her.

She walked slowly up to him her blue dress blowing in the breeze that came through. In her hair she wore one of the flowers that seemed to dance at her feet as she walked by. Finally she stood in front of him, she was even more breathtaking that he remembered. Eli felt as if his breath caught in his lungs when she looked up at him. She reached up and placed her fingers on his lips before replacing them with her own. Eli made a sound of pleasure in his throat as her lips touched his. He wrapped his arms around her pulling her close not caring that he did not know who she was. He was drowning in her exotic taste as his tongue slipped into her mouth and he felt her body mold to him. Eli was lost. She pulled away and smiled a radiant smile before turning and walking back to one of the trees. She sat there and looked over at him as if expecting him to follow her. Eli obliged and sat next to her, he stroked his hand over her hair as if to convince himself she was real. She smelled like papayas and passion fruit and Eli had the urge to touch his lips to her shoulders and taste her skin.

"Who are you?" he finally asked when he could find his voice.

"My name is Alison." That was her simple reply.

"You are the girl from the story and the legend of the Baqeu!" he exclaimed

She laughed softly. "They still tell that story? You should never believe everything you hear."

He grinned at her. "Well, you have to admit, your name, how elusive you are. For a while there I thought you couldn't speak."

"I assure you I can speak very well, both English and French."

"So why all the mystery, where are you from?" He had to ask; the cop in him, after all, loved the mystery around this.

"Some of the story is true. I am from the Baqeu tribe but…" He opened his mouth to speak but she held up a finger for silence and he promptly closed his mouth. "I was not stolen away from my parents. We believe the land is our mother and that is where we stay."

"Okay, so you live here?" he asked, gesturing to the grove around him.

"I live many places, everywhere and anywhere on the island. Some places I walk most islanders are scared to go or have never seen. This place is by far one of my favorite and my own special place," Alison said with a beaming smile. "What is your name?" Her accent was thick and sexy as hell, and Eli felt his cock harden in response.

"My name—I'm Elijah Connors, Eli."

"Elijah Connors. I like your name."

"Thank you, and I like, Alison. Now why did you kiss me?

"Because I desired to kiss you, Elijah. I think I desire to do it again, but not right now. Before I do that I am going to show you the island that no one else gets to see." She stood up and extended her hand out to him. He got up and brushed off his pants legs before enclosing her hand in his big one.

"So where is your snake?" he asked casually and she brushed vines out of their way and they began walking back to the beach.

"He is around here somewhere. He comes and goes as he pleases."

He watched as she walked into the surf and her dress became wet and clung to her body. Eli felt his body harden once again when he could make out her nipples and the secret curves of her body.

"Are you coming, Elijah?" she called to him before she dove into the surf.

"You bet your ass," he muttered before he ran down the beach. He dived into the warm water following her through the white capped waves. He felt a thrill of excitement as the water enveloped him. This adventure was just beginning.

Chapter Three

They swam a distance out into the crystal blue water. Eli was tall but his toes could barely touch the sandy bottom of the sea he looked back to the beach and could not believe how far they had swum. She faced him with a wide smile while her lithe body treaded the water gracefully.

Eli looked back to the sandy shore and then to her smiling face. "So where are we going again?"

She let her body glide through the water and she wound her arms around his neck. "Are you unsure of going with me, Elijah?"

Her body being so close to him was giving him delicious sensation and very dirty thoughts. "No. Right now I'd follow you anywhere, but humor me anyway."

"We are going down," she replied simply.

"Down? Down where?"

"Take a breath, Elijah."

He took a breath understanding her meaning. Her lips met his and Alison pulled them both under the water. Eli opened his eyes and saw fishes in arrays of vibrant colors swim pass him. The coral waved in the underwater currents. Eli knew none of the beauty he had seen on the island could not compare to what was under the Caribbean Sea. She took his hand and they began to swim under the water towards the opening of a cave. Eli could feel his lungs begging for a breath of air as they went into the mouth of the underwater rock formation. She began to swim upwards and he followed quickly knowing he needed to take a breath very soon. They two of them broke the surface of the water together. Eli could hear the breath he took into his lungs echo off the wall of the cave.

"Where are we?" he asked looking around. The cave was amazingly dry. He knew that part of it had to be on the surface of the island somewhere but the only way to get to it was from underwater.

"It is another one of my favorite places," Alison replied.

Eli watched her swim over to the edge of the pool and pulled herself up on to the cave floor. He followed suit and soon he was looking around in amazement. The walls were alive with coral that looked like live flowers. He reached out to touch one but it pulled back into the crack it was growing from, it was hiding from him. He gave a short laugh in amazement as he and the coral played a game of hide and seek before it finally let him caress its soft petals. To him it felt like velvet and when it wrapped one of its tiny tendrils around his finger he gasped in wonder.

"What is this place called?" he asked in amazement when she came over to him and handed him a towel.

"It is the Animal Flower Cave," Alison explained. "It used to be a tourist attraction of the island long ago, but they closed it because it became unstable and the entrance from the island collapsed in on itself.

"How did you find it and the coral? They hide and then come out when they don't feel threatened."

Alison laughed and the husky tone filled him with pleasure once again. "I found it long ago when I was a child. I remember going on a school trip to the cave before it collapsed and I knew there I had to be another opening so I found it." He watched as she reached out to caress the same flower he was playing with. It curled around her fingers and then as she moved her hand it seemed to imitate her movements. "It was called the Animal Flower Cave because the coral in here can live on both land and water and some say they have the basic characteristics of animals."

"What do you say about it?" Eli could tell by just listening to her speak she had a vast knowledge of the underwater world she seemed to love.

"I say they are correct. The coral here can feel pain, sense danger, or the intent to harm. See how he curls around your fingers? He knows you will not try to pluck him from his home."

"How do you know it's a he?" Eli teased.

"Because of the colors. The female species of this coral type have deeper red at the ends."

"How do you know all this stuff, Alison?" he asked in amazement.

"Because I live here and I love the water, plus I am a marine biologist at the university here on the island."

Eli knew he must have been wearing an expression of pure shock on his face because Alison broke out laughing.

"Did I ruin the mystique for you, Eli? The girl from the Baqeu tribe stolen at birth and lives alone in the gullies and caves of the island?"

"No...no I mean why do people assume that legend is real?"

She wiped tears of mirth from her eyes. "Like I said before, do not believe everything you hear. I am from the tribe, yes, but I went to school and college in America". She extended her hands. "My people and I feel very comfortable among the sea life and the in the gullies of the island but it is not our only homes. Some of us are doctors, lawyers, teachers, and we come back to this connection whenever we can." She looked at him with dark eyes. "So, Elijah Connors, have I ruined the myth for you?"

"Far from it. I think I am more intrigued than ever," he replied softly.

"Come then." She held out her hand to him and he took it and Alison led him further back into the cave. He looked around as they passed a file cabinet and a few chairs. A small desk with a kerosene lamp on it, and then in the farthest corner near the rock wall a cot where she could sleep.

"How did you get all this stuff down here?" he asked in amazement.

"I did it bit by bit with waterproof containers and the help of my brothers. I am keeping track of the coral, the climate changes, and poachers' effects on this ecosystem."

"Do you bring a lot of people down here?" he asked, sitting on the cot. He watched as she lit the few lamps she had sitting around.

"By people do you mean guys?" she asked in an amused tone. "And no. No one knows about this place but my brothers."

"Then why me, Alison?

She walked over and stood between his legs. She took his hands and placed then on her hips. "Why do you think, Elijah?" With those words she let her lips roam his softly and Eli was lost.

* * * *

Maybe it was the exotic cave filled with unimaginable wonders, or the woman standing in front of him, but Eli felt as if he was in some kind of fantasy from which he did not want to escape. Alison had the taste of mango and coconuts and as her tongue slipped inside his mouth he could not help the moan of pleasure that escaped his lips. His hands moved from where she placed them on her hip to trace the curve of her back. He lifted her easily and placed her on his lap. Alison gasped at the intimate connection. Eli was already hard and throbbing in his damp shorts. She wrapped her legs around his waist and pressed herself against his hardness. Eli groaned and he took control of the kiss, letting his fingers bury themselves in the thick tresses of her hair and devouring her lips.

He tore his mouth away from her. "Alison, I have never wanted some one this much, this quickly."

She looked into his eyes. "Then take me, Elijah. I want you, too."

Her hands roamed over the strong contours of shoulders. Her touch enflamed him as each caress was like fire against his skin. He gathered up the ends of her dress and pulled up over head, freeing her from the confines of the material. He filled his hands with the smooth globes of her breasts and watched as she arched into his palms.

"You like how my hands feel on you," he murmured with assuredness in his voice. "The way I caress your skin and touch you like this."

"Yes, yes I do, Elijah," she whispered.

His eyes widened in surprise as she pushed him back against the soft sheets on the cot. She climbed off him and flashed him a quick smile before pulling his swim trucks off. His cock was already hard when she settled herself on her knees between his legs. Eli watched her. Her hand ran down his body and caressed his chest moving slowly to the part of his body that ached to be inside her. When she took his cock in her grasp and fondled him, his breath hissed out. Eli's hips moved each time she stroked his hard length. Their eyes connected and he knew she was watching pleasure cross his face from her touch alone. Her lips descended and wrapped around the head of his cock and a low moan left his lips. She took him deeper into her mouth and Eli thought he could die from the bliss her lips and hands were creating. He couldn't stand it any longer, he pulled her roughly against his chest and took her lips in a hunger filled kiss. He let his hand slip between their bodies to her pussy. He found her slick and moist and slid his two fingers deep inside her. Her body bucked against him and she cried out at the instant rush of pleasure.

She sat up on his thighs and took his fingers deeper. He spread his legs so that her thighs were wider around his and he could watch himself use his fingers to please her. Her back was arched in pleasure and her head leaned back until he could feel her hair caress his legs.

"Ride my fingers, baby," he coaxed her softly. "Take them deep, sweetheart, oh yes like that." His thumb circled the sensitive nub of flesh in between the pink folds of her pussy.

He watched her body rise and fall, the way her thighs clenched each time her body took his digits inside her. Each time her body moved, he watched her glistening wetness drip down his fingers. Her lips were parted and tiny moans escaped.

"I'm going to come, Elijah." The exotic accent and the way she said his name drove him wild he pressed deeper inside her and used his other hand to pinch her upturned nipples sending her spiraling to orgasm. He did not wait for he to catch her breath, watching her come built him to a frenzied state. The need to bury his cock inside her went beyond reason. He pulled her down on his waiting shaft and the feeling of her hot, slick pussy enclosing around his engorged cock wrung a harsh cry from his lips. The sheer pleasure of it almost sent him into his own orgasm. He gritted his teeth as Alison began to move on her own accord. Her body writhed and slid down on his cock over and over again. He looked at her with her lips parted and her lids heavy with passion. She was in the throes of her own ardor and Eli grabbed her hips to still her movements.

"Stop, baby, stop just a minute," he groaned out, his breathing harsh.

Her body stilled but she trembled uncontrollably. "Elijah, I can't I need to move, to feel you. You are so thick I want more, please more."

"I want to make it last...." he tried to explain. "If you move I am going to lose control."

She leaned over and kissed him fiercely as her body began its sensual rhythm once again. "Don't fight it, move with me, Elijah. Let's be lost together."

He could not say no. He thrust upwards to meet her body every time she moved. Their breathing echoed throughout the caves. His fingers bit into the smooth skin of her chocolate thighs while he pounded inside her.

"I need you Elijah, now!" she cried out. Her body took up a frenzied pace. "Come with me!"

Her body clenched around him like a velvet glove and Eli felt his own orgasm begin. "Yes, baby, I'm with you!"

His groan mixed with her cries of bliss as they went over that sensual edge. She fell against his chest and his arms automatically wrapped around her cocooning her in his embrace. There in the tropical cave filled with living coral they were lost in the each other.

Chapter Four

"We have to go," Alison said softly as she caressed his chest. She knew it was well after midnight, even though they were in the cave. She did not need a clock to tell her what the time was; she was so in tune with nature she could tell. They had spent hours in the cave making love and talking softly to each other about any and everything. Alison could not deny she felt a connection with him; that was why she came back to find him. She always followed her instincts.

"Go where?" he asked sleepily.

She laughed huskily. "Back to the beach, so you can go home, your friend will worry."

"He knows I can take care of myself." Eli rolled over and pulled her into his embrace, kissing lovingly on the neck. "I want to say here with you."

Alison arched her neck in pleasure and made a purring sound at his touch. He was fogging her thoughts with his touch. "In Philadelphia yes, but not here, he will worry."

She moaned when his hand reached between them and rubbed her clit gently. She could feel his hard cock pressed against her thigh and she opened her legs wider to give him entry to her waiting pussy. He slipped inside her easily to the hilt. Making her cry out, he was so thick and filled her easily.

His breath was harsh against her ear, making her shiver while he pushed him self deeper inside her. "Just a little more, Alison. I can't seem to get enough of you."

She was already locking her legs around his waist her body rose to meet his cock and her body arched and shuddered under him. "Yes, Elijah. Yes!"

His lips roamed down her neck, and even as he thrust inside her he captured her nipple in his mouth, laving it with his tongue before suckling deeply. Alison cried out as sensation after sensation ripped through her core. She never knew pleasure this intense in her life. She didn't ever want it to stop, but she felt her release building inside her like a volcano ready to erupt.

He was pounding so hard inside her now he drove her from one orgasm to another before he spilled his seed inside her.

It was much later before they left the cave the same way they came. The water was surprisingly warm as they swam back to shore. On the beach Eli held her in his arms and Alison could tell he was as effected as she by their time together.

"Should I take you home first?" Eli asked, kissing the top of her head.

"No I can find my way very easily from here," she replied. "You remember, I know this island like the back of my hand."

"I know, I know, island girl."

Just then they heard the motor of a power boat and they watched as it pulled out of the cover further down the beach into the moonlight water. The moon was full and even from the distance Alison could tell they were two men on board.

"Wonder where they are going so late?" Eli mused.

"Poachers." Alison spat the word out like a bad taste in her mouth. "They wait until night time to go break the coral off and sell it to tourists. The reef is protected by the government and the EPA."

"Shouldn't we call some one then? Let them know?" Eli asked.

"Most of the police turn a blind eye to it because they can get a piece of the pie from the poacher. The ones who would do something by the time they get here those men will be long gone." Alison sighed as sadness ripped through her. "They don't understand unless you harvest coral the right way it kills the whole thing. They break it off the rock and then something that took hundreds of year to form dies in weeks." She knew there was venom in her voice but she felt strongly that poachers should be punished more for the destruction of the coral reef.

"Alison, don't go after those men alone. I'm a cop, and I'm telling you men like that can be very dangerous."

She reached up and kissed him gently. "I won't go after them. Let's not worry about it now, you go home."

"When will I see you again?" he asked.

"Meet me by the grove tomorrow. I will take you someplace remarkable."

"As opposed to the remarkable cave you showed me today?" he teased.

"Much better than that, I promise."

She kissed him once more and walked up the beach to the grove. She felt his eyes on her as she walked in between the trees and was swallowed by the lush grove and the darkness of the night. He walked away slowly looking back every now and again to where he saw her. Alison smiled gently; she wanted to run after him herself and not be away from him. But now she had other things on her mind at that point. She would not go after the men alone, but they would be back again that night to the cove for more coral. She would wait and see where they were taking it from off the reef and see where they were going with their precious cargo.

* * * *

"Hey, where were you, man!"

Mick's voice reached Eli's ears as soon as he walked into the kitchen. He knew he must look like a fool damp with sand covering his feet and a big grin on his face but Eli could not help it.

"I was on the beach, then in a cave, then back on the beach again."

Mick peered at him with curiosity etched on his face. "Are you drunk? I told you about those island drinks at the beach bar..."

Eli chortled with laughter before sitting down at the kitchen table. "I am far from drunk. Mick. I found that girl!"

"What girl?"

"The one I told you about that was singing to her snake. Her name is Alison and she is the same girl from Jewel's story!"

Mick looked at his excited friend. "Now I know you've been hitting the sauce, that was a myth..."

"No, it's not trust me. Mick, have you ever known me to exaggerate anything? She is as real as you and me."

"Well, you're right. I have never known you to be this excited about anything. Okay, tell me about this Alison."

"Well, parts of Jewels story are true. She is from that tribe the Baqeu but she wasn't stolen at birth. They like living off the island and trust me she knows tons about stuff I don't even recognize, and guess what: she went to school in America and she is a marine biologist." Eli leaned forward, knowing he was jabbering like an excited monkey, but he couldn't help it. "She is studying and trying to save the coral of the island. Plus she took me to this underwater cave with these amazing corals."

"Okay, man, I get your point; no one could make up a story like this." Mick held up his hand to stop Eli's flow of words. "So when do I get to meet this Alison?"

"I don't know, man, but after spending the whole evening with her in that cave and making love. I think I have fallen for her, Mick." Eli saw his friends jaw drop and his face took on a look of absolute shock.

"You made love and you think you are in love," Mick repeated slowly.

Eli leaned back in his chat with his fingers twined behind his head. "Yeah, ain't it cool or what?"

"Uh-huh, and where is Alison again?"

"She went home. We saw some poachers break off the coral at the reef and that is what she is trying to stop."

"She didn't go after them, did she? Poachers are bad news here, man."

Eli felt a sliver of fear run through him but he saw her go back into the grove so he tried to push his worry aside. "No, I saw her go and the poachers were far out to sea by the time I left her."

"Well, the next time you see your Alison bring her by the house for an introduction. I still think you might have had too much sun, but hey, that's just me." Mick said getting up. "I'm going up to bed before Jewel locks me out of the bedroom."

"Night," Eli called after him. He went back out to the door and looked up the beach. Alison was in his thoughts and a smile curved his face. He washed his feet off outside quickly and went upstairs to shower and go to bed. He wanted the night to pass quickly so he could see her again.

* * * *

Alison followed all the tracks and paths through the gullies she knew even in the dark. She wanted to get to the other side of the cove so she could see where the poachers were coming in. She needed to know which part of the reef they were destroying for profit. She had found Columbus hanging from a tree in the grove when she came back, so now he was wrapped around her body as she moved stealthily though the night. She heard the motor of their boat coming back in and she laid flat against the ground and looked over the edge of the rocks. There were two of them, one an islander, and she could tell the other was one was a tourist. They dropped the heavy anchor onto to the reef, not caring that the metal would damage even more of the coral growing there. Alison felt her anger rise. She wanted to rush down to the beach and stop them from breaking any more of the precious underwater coral. But by herself she could not do anything and her brothers were not on the island at that time. She would have to report it to the authorities in the morning. As she turned to move she moved some of the loose rocks on the ledge and sent it down to the shallow water. Even as she heard it splash and their shouts that someone was there, her heart jumped into her throat.

"Its some girl up there, man!" one of the poachers shouted. "We can go up around the bluff and cut her off."

She saw the light they were using flash up to the rocks. She hoped that she had moved quickly enough so they would not have seen her. Obviously she was not as quick as she thought.

"We'll see if you cut me off. Come on, Columbus." She took the snake up and moved quickly into the shadows. If they were coming up to the bluff to see if who was there they would not find her. She could hear their footfalls coming closer. The flower laden vines and the vegetation of the gullies seem to cover her path as she ran. One of them had a flash light and she tried to dodge the beams as they flashed while moved through the trees and plants.

Columbus was getting heavy and she stopped to put him on a low hanging tree branch. "I'll see you at home," she whispered and kissed the snake's yellow head. That was when the beam of light settled on her.

"I've found her!" a deep voice yelled. "Over here!"

The poacher dressed in a yellow Hawaiian shirt and cargo pants came towards her. She stepped back slowly, whispering words that were taught to her long ago. The words made the plants hum and whisper like a breeze moving though their branches and leaves. She watched the poacher's eyes widen as he looked around wildly as the trees moved. He lunged at her, his eyes wild with fear and anticipation of catching his prey. Before he could even touch her, vines twined around his legs and he fell with a hard thud. His angry shouts filled the air as he was pulled up into a tree and left hanging there. Alison gave her attacker an amused look before she turned on her heels and ran once more. By the time his friends found him she would be long gone for home.

Home to Alison was a two-story plantation style house made of wood and limestone. It was in complete disrepair when she found it, but she fell in love with the location and the ruined building. She bought it and, with the help of her brothers and the rest of the tribe, brought it back to its original beauty. Now she walked up the stone steps to the patio where she sat in the evening and watched the sunset. She wished she was not alone, she wished that she had brought Eli home with her. As she closed the door, she looked out into the night with a small smile. Tomorrow would be another day with him. She had patience she could wait until then.

Chapter Five

Eli was waiting at the grove by eleven the next morning. He had woken up to find what had become the usual scenario. Mick and Jewel in the kitchen eating breakfast and teasing each other.

"Good morning, Eli, would you like breakfast?" Jewel asked.

"Nope. I'm heading out early today," he said as he grabbed an orange off the table. "See you two later, have a good day, guys."

"Going to meet that girl, huh?" Mick turned to his wife. "Eli met him a girl from the Baqeu tribe named Alison, imagine that."

Jewel looked at Eli as he stood next to the door. "Be careful, Eli, this island holds more than most people think."

"Yeah. Don't I know it. See ya." He grinned at their curious expression when he left by the back door and headed down the beach. He couldn't help that he was filled with excitement and felt like a school boy ditching school. He wanted to be near Alison again, and every minute away from her felt like too much.

He stopped walking for a moment. *When did I become such a love struck fool?* Honestly, since he had been on the island he felt nothing but carefree; gone were the grim lines around his mouth and the hardened cop personality. Even when he was on the plane he felt like punching the guy across from him who kept talking loudly and laughing over drinks. Now he was practically skipping across the beach. He knew when he went back to Philly he would have to resurrect the part of him that was suppressed by the island. *I'm going to miss this,* he thought as he resumed his walk to the grove.

"Why that look on your face?" Her voice broke through to the maze of thoughts running through his head.

He turned to see her standing behind him. He was so lost in his own mind that he did not hear her walk up or she moved that quietly. She was dressed in a green dress today—the straps were thin and looked like braided gold. On her feet were sandals that matched the straps of her dress. She looked exquisite, no makeup on her face, just pure beauty that made him catch his breath.

"You look wonderful, did you go somewhere?" he said as he pulled her into his arms and inhaled the scent of her perfume. She smelled like exotic hibiscus flowers that Jewel picked from her garden every day.

"I went to the police about the poachers. Now why did you look so sad when I walked up?"

"I was thinking about having to go home and leave the island."

"And that makes you sad?"

Eli sighed. "My life back home is so tough, the choices I have to make, the things I see. Here it is so easy; being with you is so natural."

Alison reached up and caressed his face; he closed his eyes and reveled in her touch. "Don't think so much Elijah, just feel, the rest will come to you in time."

Their lips met in a soft kiss that made Eli feel things that he thought were long lost inside him. This was more than a tryst with an island girl, this was magic.

"So what did the police say about the poachers?" he asked, nibbling on her lips.

Alison made a soft sound of pleasure in her throat. "As usual they can do nothing, but I have a plan to stop them."

"Whoa there, you are not going after those guys. Do you understand me! Mick said they are dangerous and…"

She pulled out of his arms, her eyes flashing fire. "No, it is you who does not understand, Elijah! If the reef dies, the sea life dies, the ecosystem is destroyed! It affects tourism, and fishing. It is like building a house of cards, if one part falls all of it falls!"

He pulled her back into his arms roughly. "I won't have you being hurt! I couldn't stand the thought of you being hurt!" Emotion made his voice break and Alison searched his eyes.

"I care for you, too," she whispered softly. She smiled bright at him and changed the conversation. "I promised you a surprise, didn't I, are you ready to go see it?"

"Yes, let's go see this surprise. Can we pick up something to eat along the way?"

Alison laughed as they walked through the grove hand in had. "Sure, we can eat along the way."

Her version of picking up something to eat was not stopping at a local restaurant. It was to pick fruit along the path they walked on. Mangoes, papaya, oranges, pineapples and so much more all grew wild throughout the island. Eli followed behind her on a winding path and then went down a steep hill into a cavern carved out of the rocks. Eli could hear the trickle of water. The light that came through from the other side of the cavern showed the stream that run down the limestone.

Finally she looked back at him and smiled. "Here it is."

Eli came to stand beside her. The view in front him was striking. There were no words to describe the beauty spread out before him. The gully was filled with birds of unimaginable colors flying from branch to branch. From where they stood he saw a waterfall cascading down from the rocks into a crystal pool beneath.

"This is amazing!" he exclaimed.

"It gets better, come on," she encouraged him and stared down the steps carved out of the rocks to the gully floor. Soon they were standing next to the roaring waterfall. Alison stripped her dress off and then her lacy green panties. Eli felt desire shot through him as he watched her jump into the water.

She came up and wiped the water from her face. "Are you going to just stand there or are you going to join me?"

He needed no more of an invitation than that; in a few seconds he was nude and diving into the cool clear water.

He came up right next to her and pulled her instantly into his arms. Wet slick bodies rubbed together as they treaded water, and their lips met and devoured each other in a kiss.

"You looked like a water nymph when you rose out of the water. I wonder if you are a Siren that cast a spell over me," he whispered as he looked at her.

"Would it be easier if you believed that, Elijah? Would you stay if I asked you to?"

"I don't know what I would do, Alison. All I know is I can't seem to stop smiling when I am near you and the thought of leaving on a plane without you is something I don't want to fathom. Come with me?" he asked impulsively. It was true, when it was time for him to go. His world would become bleak without her.

"Let's not think right now," she whispered. Alison kissed him once more; Eli let himself be lost in her kiss.

Her legs wrapped around his waist and she pressed herself against his throbbing cock. Eli groaned and stood on the cool rock floor of the pool. He reached between their bodies and let his cock sink deep inside her. She pressed kisses along his neck and bit his ear gently. He felt himself shudder as he thrust himself deeper inside her. Her soft cries of ecstasy were muffled against his neck.

"*Je'temme*, Elijah, *Je'temme*." Her words ended on a moan while her hands buried in his hair and her body locked around his. They made love in the pool while the sounds of the waterfalls mixed and blended wit their voices as pleasure overtook them.

He walked out of the pool with his cock still buried inside her and laid her against the soft grass. With her body under him he caught her nipple between his lips. He wanted to engorge himself with her taste, imprint the feel of her body wrapped around him to his memories. She was so soft, so wet wrapped around his shaft. Each time he slid inside her, she moaned or sighed his name. It made him feel like he was the only man in the world. It made him feel loved.

His cock throbbed as their pace increased and soon their cries were echoed by the mockingbirds on the island. Her hands clenched on the taut muscles off his ass while her hips rose and fell in frenzy. Her release erupted and his cock pulsed inside her while his lips were against the soft skin of her neck. Her hands did not stop touching him. She caressed his back and his neck, whispering something her could not understand in his ear.

The spent the rest of the day frolicking in the pool and under the waterfall, running through the forest and the trees and eating fruits he had never even heard of. She even showed him how to suck the sweet juice from sugar canes and laughed at him when it dribbled down his chin. By the time the sun began to set and the shadows of evening crossed the tree tops, he was as contented as he could possibly be.

"Why do you seem so unhappy when you think about leaving the island, Elijah? What happened there to make you so sad?" Alison asked softly.

Eli sighed. "It's not just one thing, it's a combination of so much. I have been a cop for fifteen year, and in that time I have seen women sell their children for drugs, men beating their women to death. Senseless murders and children dead on the streets. And no matter what I do it seems as if I am not even making a dent. I jut don't know if I can do it anymore."

"I can't even fathom what you go through everyday. I wish I could ask you to stay, but that would not be fair."

"You want me to stay?" He turned to her and caressed her soft cheek.

"I cannot ask you to do that for me," Alison said, kissing his palm. "However jaded your life is there, you make a difference and they need you, just like I am needed here."

"Hmmpphhhh," Eli grumbled good-naturedly. "So you say, but a life of decadence on the island sounds good to me."

Alison laughed softly. "Come, we won't go home just yet. I'll show you something not even the islanders get to see."

"What else could there be?"

"You'll see," she replied mysteriously.

DAHLIA ROSE

Chapter Six

Alison led him deeper into the gully of the island. When he looked up he could see a small rope bridge old and decayed with the rotted wood slats. Above that bride was another bridge built with cement pillars and steel beams, he could barely make out the truck and cars passing on it. How far down into the belly of the tropical paradise were they, he wondered to himself. He could almost picture the older generation of islanders traveling on that old rope crossing to get from one place to another.

"My mother told me once that my grandfather used to cross that shaking old thing everyday to carry sugar cane to the mills." Alison's soft words broke into his thoughts. She had so much heritage on the island, generation after generation of her family were born and died there. He wished he felt that kind of connection to something. Being alone all his life, from foster home to foster home and then straight to the police department when he could apply. Eli could only call police work his family. He shook his head, knowing that the only pictures in his cramped apartment were the ones he bought to hang on his walls. There were no family photos to look at fondly, no treasured knickknacks that were passed down.

"You're making that face again, Elijah," Alison said softly. She stopped to stare at him. "No unhappy thoughts, you find your home when it is time."

"Reading my mind, Alison?" He bent and kissed her full lips.

"No, reading your heart." Her words made that said organ jump in his chest. "Let's go before we are late."

Eli nodded and she let her hand slip around his waist as they walked. Soon he could hear the faint sound of music and drums coming through the trees to his ears. The deeper they walked into the dense woods the louder the music became, he could hear the sound of the steel drums and pipes. Eli pushed back leafy palm fronds, and he and Alison entered a clearing with torches that lined the outside. People milled around, eating, drinking, and laughing, and all turned when they saw Alison come out of the woods. Eli could feel the stares as she smiled and kissed cheeks of the people he assumed was her tribe.

One man stood out from the others. He was tall and his brown shoulders were broad. He was dressed in simple slacks and a crisp white cotton shirt, but his feet were bare. As they walked up to him Alison reached out and embraced him over her shoulders. He met Eli's eyes with a questioning look.

"Alison, I did not know you were coming tonight, and who is this with you?" The man's voice rumbled from his chest.

"Papa, this is Elijah, my new friend." Alison said as she pulled Eli next to her.

"Must be more than a friend to bring him tonight, eh?" Alison's father looked from him to her.

"I'll be back," Alison said and kissed her father's cheek before kissing Eli's and walked away.

"It's nice to meet you, sir," Eli cut in and met his stare. Her father was a formidable man, and Eli could tell most men would be afraid of him, he was not most men.

"Welcome to the Baqeu tribal dance, Elijah. Eat, drink, and join the revelry with us. I am Joseph, her father." He looked Eli from top to bottom and his face split into a wide grin, showing of the whiteness of his teeth in

40

the waning light. "You must be very important to Alison if she brought you tonight; she never comes to this dance anymore. All the others, but never this one."

"Why is that, sir?" Eli asked curiously. Alison had gone of with some women. Her father promptly pushed a cup into his hand and he took a sip and coughed. A big loud laughed erupted from her father as he heartily slapped Eli on the back.

"Call me Joseph. Too much rum, eh? I told them too much rum in the coconut milk, they never listen." They began to walk over to a table filled with breads, meats, rice and deserts while Joseph spoke. "Oh yes, why she brought you tonight? You tell me, Elijah? After all, this is the new moon ritual for love."

Eli's mouth fell open as he watched her father walk away with a smile on his face and his hands in his pockets. *New moon love ritual?* He had no more time to think of the implications as people came around him and the introductions to the Baqeu tribesmen and women began.

* * * *

The sunset turned to night, and Eli was in the middle of one of the deepest gullies of the island with a tribe of people the islanders called a myth. He had met so many of them that his head was spinning trying to remember names, or was it the rum in the coconut milk? He did not really care, he was having the time of his life. He had met one of her brothers—the other one was in London finishing up exams. Aunts, uncles, nieces, nephews, children and adults, they were all there and Eli was sure he met them all.

Alison herself seemed to be amazed at how much the tribe had grown. He had a full stomach filled with roasted meats and fish, and when everyone started to sit down he looked around for his host who seemed to have disappeared suddenly.

"Sit, Elijah." He father's voice came up behind him and he ushered Eli to an empty mat on the soft grass.

The music changed from party-like to something slow and sensual. Women ushered the little ones away and Eli felt his heart thump with anticipation when he saw Alison appear with a group of other young women. Eli looked around at the group of young men he was sitting with, who smiled and clapped eagerly as the women came out. Eli had eyes only for one of them.

They wore almost nothing across their bodies, just a bikini in a blue shimmering wrap that looked as delicate as spider webs. The women began their slow movements to the rhythm of the music that played around them. Their hips gyrated from side to side and they beckoned the men to them with slender arms. Each girl chose the man whom she danced in front of, and Alison chose Eli. His eyes followed the curves of her body, noting how the firelight of the torches seemed to glow off her skin and trail down her back as she danced. She held out her hand to him and Eli gladly accepted. They walked over to where her father sat and she kissed his cheek gently.

"Bye, papa," she whispered softly.

The older man nodded at Eli as they walked past him back into the woods of the gully where the path was now illuminated by moonlight.

"That was unbelievable, Alison! The music, the people, it is amazing that know one knows your tribe does this down here."

"No one can see from the bridge above, and the people here are scared of the gullies, especially at night." She laughed softly. "I'm glad you like my family. You see we are not the myth that everyone thinks."

"You're a myth to me, mixed with mystery and spiced with sexuality. I have never met anyone like you!" Eli said it reverently. She had consumed his every thought until there was not a moment spent that he did not think of her.

She pulled him off the path into a stand of trees and began kissing him feverishly. Eli returned her kisses with just as much excitement. She was in his blood like the rum he had been drinking. He tore his lips away from hers and began to kiss his way down her neck. His hands reached behind her and untied the delicate strings of her top before filling his palms with the smooth globes of her breasts. Eli took the upturned nipples into his mouth and laved each with his tongue before sucking deeply and causing her to cry out in pleasure.

"I can't seem to get enough of your taste!" he whispered. "I need to taste all of you, can I, Alison?"

"Yes. Oh yes, Elijah!"

"I love how you say my name," he said as he kissed his way down her body.

His lips trailed down her smooth abdomen and across the curve of her thigh, and he pulled her bikini bottoms down to her ankles. She stepped from them easily and spread her legs to allow him access to what he sought. He felt her tremble when his hot breath met the soft skin of her pussy. When his tongue flicked between the folds of sweet flesh her hips jerked in response. Eli could not stand the teasing himself, with a rough jerk he brought her hips to him and pressed his lips against her pussy. Alison's cry shattered the quiet around them while his tongue licked and sucked at the sensitive bud of her clit before burying inside her. Her hips undulated against his face until her body shook with her release. He was on his feet before she could even catch her breath, and Eli was hurriedly unfastening his ants and pushing then down his legs. He wanted to be inside her, to feel her wrapped around his cock. He could never get enough of the sensation of her body pulling his in deeper. He took her legs and wrapped them around his waist, sinking his cock inside her wet pussy.

His groan of pleasure was muffled against her neck. He whispered into her ears, "You feel so good, baby, so damn good. Take more of me sweetheart, ah, just like that."

Alison arched in pleasure, pressed against the smooth bark of the tree. "Oh please, Elijah, I need you!"

"You have me, sweetheart, always!" He could feel his own orgasm take hold as he pounded inside her furiously. Each thrust sent them both higher and higher until their cries blended into one. He sunk to his knees with Alison still in his arms, holding her tight against him and whispering to her. She in turn kissed every spot of his body she could reach and echoed his words. If this was not heaven, Eli did not know what was. This was love, he was so certain of it now more than he ever was about anything in his life. How could he leave her when it was time to go home?

Chapter Seven

They walked hand in hand back through the cavern and back to the grove on the beach. The night was clear, and as they walked out to the beach they let the waves wash up on their feet. The couple did not see the men coming up from the water until the very last moment. In their hands they carried netted bags full of broken coral poached off the reef. Their eyes met with Eli's and Alison's, and for an instant it seemed as if time stood still.

"It's the bitch from last night," the man snarled.

"Yes, it's me, and I see you have been at it again, killing the reef for a few dollars," Alison said defiantly.

After I told her not to follow them! Eli thought as he watched the men move closer up from the wave line.

"How much did you break off from the reef tonight, three hundred dollars worth, maybe more!" Alison cried out. "Can't you see you are destroying more than rocks, you are destroying our tourist industry. What will visitors come to see, but empty sand with no fish or sea life!"

"Alison, please be quiet," Eli said gently. He knew that the odds were stacked against them, and aggravating the men could only make the situation worse. He looked for a route of escape. The men stood between them and the grove, the next choice was the sea but they had no boat. They were essentially trapped.

"Listen, lady, we all got to survive, one way or another. Now we have to do what we have to do to keep your mouth shut." The man holding the spear gun smiled cruelly.

Eli felt the danger around them, and he instinctively pulled Alison closer to his side.

"Listen, guys, we didn't see a thing. Just me and my girl coming home from a nice evening, no harm no foul." Eli tried to reason with them.

"See, the damn tourists even come and take our women," the other poacher said. "She thinks she's too good for us islanders now, eh."

Alison tsked softly. "Gentlemen, I and every other woman on this island are too good for a bunch of low class poachers like you."

"Bitch...!" the man snarled.

"Alison…" Eli tried to warn her. But she went on speaking, unhearing of the words. Eli could see now why Mick said the women of the island were headstrong. She was mad as hell, and the fire of anger lit her eyes.

"Yes, I'm a bitch, a bitch that is gong to report you to the Commissioner, not the lowly constable of this beach you can buy off."

The threat of impending imprisonment was all it took. Eli knew the criminal mind and he knew these men would look at self preservation over human life. The man who held the spear gun raised it again, and this time he fired it at them. Eli pushed Alison to the sand and he felt the searing pain as the spear hit his arm and tore through his flesh. Not thinking of the pain, he pulled her to her feet and began to run down the beach. The waves crashed against their legs and they tried to fight the current coming to get deeper into the water.

"Elijah! You're bleeding!" she cried out in alarm. Alison tried to stop to look at him but he could hear the roar of the jet skis as they tried to cut them off by water.

"We have to get you to your friend's house!" She tried to stop the heavy flow of blood. Eli gritted his teeth as her hands touched the wound, but his skin was ripped apart by the steel blade meant to kill barracudas and sharks.

He pulled her down by the rocks as the poachers passed. "Mick's house is too far, baby. They are going to double back when they don't see us."

"The cave, we have to go to the cave! Can you dive?" she asked urgently.

Eli could feel the blood oozing from the deep wound down his arms. He looked at his arm, they had not cut a vein but the wound was deep enough that it kept bleeding. Already he could feel himself getting weak, but he knew they had no choice. "I can dive, baby, you just lead the way."

She took the glittering wrap she danced with earlier and tied it tightly around his arms, trying to stop the flow of blood. "Barracudas they are like sharks. Blood brings them coming to feed," she explained.

He winced and grimaced in pain as she tied his arm tight, the pain almost making his pass out. The sound of the jet skis were getting louder once again so they hurried further out into the water.

Before she took her deep breath, Alison held his face between her hands and kissed him hard. "I love you!" she said fiercely.

"God, Alison. I'm glad you said that because I love you, too!" he replied and kissed her again hard and as if this would be last time he would ever taste her lips.

They took a breath and sank under the warm Caribbean Sea. As they swam below, the bubbles from the propeller were above, circling. Eli felt himself losing the battle to stay conscious. The loss of blood made him weak. As he lagged back Alison felt the pull of his weight. She looked back and the last thing he remembered was seeing her face take on a look of alarm as darkness claimed him.

* * * *

Reality surged through Eli, taking him from unconsciousness in seconds. He sat up, coughing up the salt water in his lungs. *How long was I out?* He did not have time to think because Alison launched herself in his arms and sobs racked her body.

"I thought you were gone! I thought you were gone!" she repeated, raining kisses on his face."

His arm throbbed painfully, but he hugged her as tight as he could. "I'm okay, baby. I'm okay. How did you get me up here?"

"A dolphin I know helped me pull you up to the pool." She tried to smile through her tears.

"You're kidding!" he said in amazement, but sucked in his breath once more as a pain shot through is arm.

"No, I am not." She untied his arm gingerly looking at the gash as it still bled. "You won't be able to go back down, I am going to have to leave you here and go get help."

"No! I can't let you go back up there alone!"

"What other choice do we have, Elijah? Even if they are gone you cannot dive. I have to go and get help!"

He started to protest but he knew she was right. He sighed. "Go to Mick. He'll get be the one to get things done quickly. Do you know how to get to the house?" he asked as she helped him lay on the cot.

She smiled. "This my island, remember? I always knew where you lived." She kissed him gently. "Rest. I'll be back soon." He watched her as she slipped back in the pool and out of sight quickly.

"I love you," he whispered. He knew the minutes would tick away like hours until she came back. If those men caught her and touched her, he would stay on the island and hunt them down himself.

* * * *

By the time she came up the rain was pouring. She surfaced to big droplets hitting the water and her face. She looked through the sheets of water, trying to see the shore but could not. She would have to be very careful to go in the right direction before she started swimming. If not, she could get caught in rip tides that were known to be around sometimes and be pulled farther out to sea.

She needed help. Alison closed her eyes and tapped against the water over and over again. Finally she got the response she was looking for, the fin of a dolphin cutting through the seas. She took a breath and went underwater to greet the friendly gray face. She grabbed hold of his fin and he pulled her through the water until she came up close to the beach. She rubbed his smooth head before heading for shore making note to look out for jet skis on the sand.

She spotted the small crafts pulled high on the sand. Their individual footprints headed into the grove. They thought she and Eli were hiding there, which gave her the perfect opportunity for her to find Mick and get help. The poachers had left their ill gotten treasure in the netted bags on the beach. The coral was already dead and she felt a pang of sadness for their destruction. That was not the issue. Elijah needed help. She picked up one of the bags as proof for Elijah's friend and ran up the beach as fast as she could.

She saw the house on the bluff and she never stopped running, even as her lungs burned with exertion. She took the stone steps two at a time until she came to the kitchen door. She banged and screamed Mick's name at the top of her lungs until she saw a light go on and two fingers approached behind the decorative glass.

"Child, what are you doing out in this?" the woman asked with concern in her eyes. "Why are you screaming my husband's name?" She pulled Alison out of the rain and she tried to catch her breath.

"Are you Alison?" Mick asked.

"Yes..." She gulped "Yes, I am. Elijah is hurt, poachers..." she dropped the bag at her feet.

"Don't tell me you two went after those fools yourselves," Mick said angrily, pulling on his shoes. "I told him that was danger..."

"No, we were coming home! We didn't see them coming in from the reef! One shot a spear gun and Elijah got hurt. We hid and he is too weak to get here."

"Where did you hide, in the grove?"

"No, underwater cave! Please, you must come!" she said urgently and turned to run back out the door.

Mick grabbed her arm and stopped her before she ran back out in the rain. "No, I'll call for help. He is safe until we get there, right?"

Alison nodded, she wanted to go back for Elijah but she knew his friend was correct. They would need more help to get him. Everything went by in a blur, from Mick making calls to get the police and a few of his men to come to the beach, to his wife Jewel offering her a towel and hot tea. Alison barely listened, she had to get back to Elijah, he was the only thing on her mind.

Finally they were heading back, speeding across the wet sand in dune buggies on the beach. Mick was strapping on an oxygen tank.

"There is one for you, too," he said to Alison

"I don't need one. I can get there," she said and walked into the water. She noticed his surprised look but he said nothing. Mick and two other men followed her in to the water, and soon they were heading back to where Elijah was hidden.

Please be okay, she thought as she dove deep to go to her love.

* * * *

The cave was deathly quiet except the occasional sound of water dropping in to the pool from the cave rook. He didn't notice the last time how a person could lose perception of time. His arm was still bleeding, but it had lessened considerably. He sat on the edge of the rock floor, not being able to lay in the cot another second. He was practically frantic when the hours went by and she had not returned. With many horrible images going through his head, he was just about to slide his body back in the pool to go back to get her when he saw bubbles breaking the still water and she surfaced.

"Oh my God, Alison! I was going to come after you!" He reached out his good arm and practically plucked her out of the water. He held onto him tightly just to feel her body close to him.

"I brought help, Elijah!" she said excitedly.

Mick surfaced right after her, and then the two other men. Eli could see on their faces that they were amazed at the sight and the things she had in the cave.

"Hey, man, the cavalry is here," Mick grinned when he took off his mask. "Trust you to come to an island and still find trouble."

Eli kept his arm around her. "This time it happened to find me."

"Let's get you patched up and back to dry land," Mick said and looked at his arm. "Ah shit, this is deep, man." He and his men bandaged Eli's arm as best they could and one of them buddy-breathed with Eli until they reached the surface and the sandy shore. The police were waiting on the beach; somewhere in that time Alison managed to slip away quietly without any one noticing. He did, but with everyone around it was hard to even get to her in time before she slipped into the grove.

"Alison! Alison!" he called out to her, but either she did not hear him over the people on the beach or she did not want to hear him. He could understand her wanting be out of the securitizing gaze of the police and the questions they would have. She wanted to protect the privacy of her cave and her people as much as possible. He wanted to go after her and protested even as Mick sat him took him to go get stitched up at he hospital.

Later that night, after his trip to the local infirmary and tons of questions from everyone, he finally had some peace. He had convinced Mick to make up a story about how they hid and where they were found. Mick finally went to bed and Eli lay across his bed with the breeze blowing through the French doors. He thought he heard singing in the wind, but passed it off as wishful thinking.

There it is again! It was distinct and he knew the voice. *Alison!* He rushed out of the door, and he did not have to go far. She was sitting on the bluff near the steps. He sat next to her and they said nothing for what seemed to be minutes.

"You will be leaving soon," she said in a matter-of-fact voice.

"Do you want to come with me?" he asked quietly, hoping her answer would change.

"I can't, Elijah. I visit America to hear lectures and attend conferences, but this is my home. My work is here." He heard the sadness in her voice.

"What if I stay here?"

She turned to him. "I could never ask you to give up your life to be here with me. I told you that, even though I love you I can't ask that of you."

"What life, Alison? I go to work, I see people do gut wrenching things, and I come home to an empty apartment feeling cold and dead inside. I lived and felt more with you in the last few days that I have in years! Why should I have to give that up?" He grabbed her by the shoulders and looked into her eyes. "You said you loved me. Did you mean it?"

"Yes, I meant it with all that is in me. I love you, Elijah." Her soft simple reply filled his heart with joy.

"I love you, too; this is a new beginning for me, a new frontier, living a paradise with the woman that I have fallen in love with. Ask me to stay Alison and I will." He was never surer of anything than he was tonight.

"Stay, Elijah," she whispered. "Stay."

He nodded and a smile curved his lips before she crushed her to him and kissed her.

"Elijah, your arm," she said around her laughter.

"I have my island girl in my arms, what better medicine is there than that?"

Eli found a new home and a new love on the beaches of Barbados. The lovers held each other while the waves broke on the beach and sealed new promises with a kiss.

Epilogue

Torches and lanterns hung from the trees, giving the Barbados night and extra glow. The sun had gone down only an hour ago and the sky still held the color of red trying to hold the twilight at bay. Decorations hung from every open apace and a table covered with food stood to one side. Alison open the door of her house and saw Eli standing there, looking out across the grass. She wrapped her arms around his waist and placed her head against the cool crisp white shirt he was wearing.

"Everyone will be arriving soon for the ceremony. Are you nervous?" she asked softly.

The ceremony was their marriage; it would be preformed in the ways and tradition of the Baqeu people. Her father would join them in the hand fasting ritual. They had already been married by a justice of the peace, but Eli wanted to do this for her and her people as well. She was so happy he was willing to embrace her traditions as well.

"Why should I be nervous? I already married you and I'd do it as many times as needed just to be with you," he replied.

"Then what are you thinking?" Alison asked softly.

"I'm at peace, honey. For the first time in a long time I don't feel as if I don't have hope. I came here and I found you, and you fixed something inside me I didn't even think was broken. It had to be that way for me to survive, to be a cop, and now I can be so much more." He turned to her as he spoke and wrapped her in his arms.

Alison rose up on her toes and kissed Eli. "I believe destiny sent you here to me, you are my love, Eli Connors."

"And you are my love, Alison, my bewitching beauty that has legends built around her name. If I didn't know better I'd still believe you are magic, baby."

Alison raised her eyebrow at him. "So you don't believe in magic anymore, hmmmmmm?"

She took his hands and led him down the limestone steps to stand on the grass between the trees. She wrapped her hands round him once more and looked up at him, waiting for his answer.

"Honey, I know the myth behind the story now, finding you was magic in itself to me. But the story about your family and spells and magic, well, that's just folklore of the island." Eli grinned and kissed her on her nose. "I'm an islander now, not a naive tourist anymore."

"Oh, you are an islander now, my Eli, but you are still naïve," Alison said softly. She began to whisper soft words, feeling Eli's curious gaze on her. As she said the last simple chat she raised her hand and the sky began to rain big, lush beautiful blooms. The trees shook their blossoms to the ground and Eli stood in the midst of it with a look of pure astonishment on his face as the island rained paradise down all around him.

"How... How are you doing that?" he exclaimed.

"Seem to me there's still a bit of magic after all." Her tinkling laughter filled the night before Alison pulled him to her for one more kiss and held him tight while the blooms of the island fell to the ground like a carpet around their feet.

When Love Commands

Prologue

Music blasted all around him through a small radio connected to big speakers. The bass was even too much still, and the sound was scratchy as one song sang *smack that all on the floor*. Sergeant Daniel Butler walked around the FOB and watched the soldiers play. It had been a long few months embedded in the middle of the war. His men had run so many missions without a break that he'd begged his commander for a little R & R. Finally they got it and what did the boys think up, a beach party in the middle of the desert. There was food on the table under the tent and it looked surprisingly good as Daniel passed by. There were thick sandwiches, fried chicken, coleslaw, and even potato salad and hot dogs. He made a mental note to come back and gorge himself soon before the pack ate everything.

Bottles of Snapple chilled in big plastic buckets and he snagged one. He turned, watching the party around him as his men cut loose and released built up stress. Their version of a beach party was to have him requisition wading pools and children's floaters. His face broke out into a grin as one of his men jumped out of the small wading pool with a yellow rubber duck tube around his waist. He was not the only one dressed in green camo boxer shorts and wearing children's floatation devices. They threw big beach balls at each other and danced to the music blaring from the intercom.

Big dumb kids, he thought and laughed out loud when one of the men got hit in the head with a red ball and chased his friend down and tackled him to the dry desert sand. While others sat in that same sand building castles of a big penis and vagina. They were having fun and that was all that mattered. In the middle of this one hundred and twenty-five-degree heat and the danger they faced every day, they had to find their fun whenever they could.

"Looks like they raided a sandbox at a porn store."

Daniel looked in the direction of the soft female voice. "Yeah, their minds are in the gutter."

"Well, at least they are getting it out creatively."

Daniel chortled. "Creatively, uh-huh, sure."

She laughed and took his Snapple from him, taking a long drink and handing it back. "Raspberry, nice flavor, and I was trying to be nice, the big cock and balls is a little disconcerting."

"Hell, it's giving me a serious case of penis envy." Her laughter was infectious and Daniel smiled before he took a sip from the Snapple bottle. He found himself wishing she had left her taste on the rim of the glass. "Honestly, the guys needed it, too many missions, one too many explosions, they needed the break."

"We all did, it seems, I've been seeing too many injuries in the med-tent lately," she replied.

"So you're a medic?"

She took his drink once more. "Um-hmmm." The noise was an affirmative to his question.

Daniel studied her soft features under the boonie hat. He wondered what her hair looked like. Her mouth looked full around the glass bottle and he thought about the taste of the raspberry tea against her lips. *You've been in country way too long, buddy.*

"Well, I gotta get back to work, you guys enjoy your beach party," she said and began to walk away.

"Hey, wait, take some food for later. Trust me, by the time you come back it will be a paper plate and crumbs here." He rushed over to the table and piled a little bit of everything onto a plate and walked it over to her. "I'm sure there are places in the med unit to keep this cool."

"Yup, they sure do. Thanks for the food."

"So, you're not going to tell me your name?" Daniel asked.

"Not now, maybe next time, soldier." Her smile was soft and he could see the hint of flirtation in her eyes.

Daniel watched her walk away with a smile of his own on his face. It would definitely be his pleasure to find out the name of the lovely medic.

* * * *

Two weeks later...

Medic! Medic! The word was being yelled over and over again by the nurse who had his hand pressed against the bleeding soldier's chest. The barrage of mortars had begun unexpectedly in the middle of the night when the camp was asleep. Then all hell broke loose. Soldiers were running all over the camp trying to get to their positions of cover. There they would return fire to the unknown enemy hidden in the darkness. Commands were being shouted out by superior officers. And there in the infirmary they were dealing with the wounded that were caught in the mayhem. Major Claire Kirkland moved quickly in the direction of the voice yelling for a medic. All the rest of her nurses were busy and the mortar fire would not stop raining down on their camp.

Claire's tour of duty had started fifteen months ago, and she was stationed at Camp Eisenhower in Baghdad, Iraq. Before that, she was deployed she was the head of Emergency Care in Washington, D.C. at the Walter Reed Medical Center. She would be again when her tour was up and she could retire. The days were hot and the temperature could rise to over a hundred and twenty degrees in the shade. The nights didn't bring much relief. If the mercury fell to a hundred degrees at night, everyone in the camp counted it as a blessing. Now, in the middle of the night with sweat soaking through her t-shirt and uniform, she ran toward the nurse who was yelling for help.

"What do you need, Private?" she addressed the male nurse in a crisp voice.

"Ma'am, his chest won't stop bleeding!" he replied.

"Listen, Pierce, you know how to deal with this in your sleep by now," Claire said exasperatedly. She looked at the wound—it wasn't deep. "Look, it's slowing down. Drop a few stitches in this guy and bandage the wound, then get him ready for transport out when this shit stops. Understood?" Claire knew she sounded bitchy and mean. But, she had no time to stop and hold his hand. War was hell. It was like the world was coming down around their ears when each mortar hit the ground.

Private Pierce's shoulders straightened with her words. "Ma'am, yes, ma'am!"

Claire nodded and went off in another direction. Before she could move two steps another wounded was brought inside. This one was bad, she could see it almost instantly. The soldier that carried the injured man over his shoulder was already soaked with blood.

"Put him down here," she ordered, pointing to an open cot.

The soldier put him down carefully into the waiting bed and Claire began working furiously cutting off his uniform. His nametag said Sergeant First Class Daniel Butler, the man she'd met at the beach party a few weeks earlier. The wounds were bad, the one on his chest had shrapnel stuck inside the torn flesh, and the gash on his head was bleeding profusely. Claire had seen him around camp, and even after the beach party she still didn't know his name, until now. A brief nod if they passed each other in the mess hall since then and a sexy smile every now and again, and that was it. Time was an issue in the middle of a war and every time she thought, *maybe I'll go talk to him the next time I see him*, it never happened. She always thought of him as handsome with nice green eyes—now, as he lay there bleeding, she could only think of his wounds.

"How did he get hit, soldier?" Claire asked as she turned to call one of her nurses over. "I'm going to need a chest tube, and hang two pints of O neg and one of platelets. He's losing blood fast. We don't have time to match him." Back to the soldier, she said, "Well, answer, how did he get hit?"

"Ma'am, he's our commander. He was trying to get one of the injured guys to cover when a mortar dropped a few feet away. They both went flyin', ma'am. The other guy didn't get up, he was gone, but I could hear the sergeant here moaning. So I went out and got him and brought him here."

She looked at him—his leg was bleeding. He probably didn't feel it with all the endorphins running though his body.

"Very brave of you, soldier," Claire commended him. "You're hurt, too. Your leg needs to be looked at. Go sit down before you fall down."

"Ma'am, not until I know that the sergeant is going to be okay."

"He is going to be fine, I'll make sure of it," Claire said firmly. "Now go get patched up, that's an order."

The soldier limped off slowly, casting backward glances to where his fallen leader lay.

The mortar fire had finally stopped, and the silence was now just as deafening as the explosions before it. Soldiers then began to move, quickly accessing damage and gathering the wounded or the dead. Claire worked quickly to put the chest tube in his side. She had to stabilize him. She watched the blood bubble from the wound in his chest. He would need surgery to fix his lung and whatever internal injuries the explosion had caused. And she knew he had to have a concussion. God, she hated this, she hated watching these guys get hurt and then have to come back and do it all over again. The ones that weren't badly injured, she would patch up. They would get a few days leave before going back to regular duties. What was leave in this hell? A few days of sleep on a hard cot, where the air-conditioning units barely made the heat bearable? She knew it was their duty, all of them, to be here, but they all were missing home. Her time was up, and Claire was ready to leave this place.

Sergeant Butler began to moan and thrash around on the cot. "Hold him down! And push five of morphine now!"

As the pain medication entered his system, his movements quieted but he was still conscious. Claire needed him that way so he did not slip into a coma, she couldn't give him any more pain meds. She didn't know how bad the concussion was and with any more he could fall asleep and never wake up.

"Sergeant Butler, can you hear me?" Claire asked as she worked on him. "I need you to respond to me if you can hear me."

"I...I hear you. Where am I?" His voice rasped out softly, he moaned again.

"You are in Medical," Claire replied. "I need for you to open your eyes for me, Sergeant."

When she got no response, she tried again with more force. "Sergeant, I need your eyes open now! Daniel, open your eyes, that's an order!"

"Yeah, yeah, don't shout," Daniel mumbled. He groggily opened his eyes. "Am I dead? There are a lot of angels over me."

"Definite concussion, double vision," Claire confirmed to the nurse next to her after checking his eyes. "No, Sergeant, you are not dead, just hurt really badly. We're going to get you on the next transport to Germany and they'll take care of you and have you better than ever."

"I want to stay here with you. You're pretty," he mumbled, blinking against the bright lights. "I remember you from the party…Al'sss…ways thought you were pretty."

Claire smiled. His speech was beginning to slur, the concussion and the morphine made this big guy say some strange things. "Don't worry, Daniel, I'll find you when you are better."

"S'okay," he said and closed his eyes.

Claire left orders with the nurse to wake him every half hour and call her if his situation changed. She went off to work on other patients who were hurt in the attack on their camp. When the skies were clear and they were given the go ahead, transport helicopters were called in to fly the wounded out. In all there were fifteen wounded and seven dead. Claire thought of the families that would see a car drive up to their homes to tell them their loved ones died honorably in battle. The feeling of loss and grieving would be great.

This was her last tour in the Army. It paid for her going to med school. She had joined the Army right after high school, convincing her mother that she wanted to join up at eighteen. Right after boot camp there were pre-med classes and course requirements. She did her residency right on base at Fort Ord in California, becoming number one in her class and sought after by a few high ranking hospitals in the country. None of their offers could pull her away from being a doctor taking care of soldiers that became like her family. Until the perfect offer came along, the one she could not refuse in Washington at one of the top military hospitals in the country.

She was there for two years before her deployment to the war zone in Iraq. Every year she worked as a doctor on base or deployed counted on her service record, and she was proud of what she had become.

Claire shook her head as tiredness took hold of her body. Even though she loved the military life, she was glad that she was going to get to retire. She could not bear to think of her mother hearing how she died honorably in some unknown country. Yes, it was time for her to give up this life.

She watched as Sergeant Daniel Butler was loaded on one of the first choppers out. His condition had improved, but he was still in serious condition. She yelled his status out to the medic on board over the whirling sound of the blades and handed the medic Daniel's chart. Even though twelve hours before he was lying on a cot with serious injuries, Daniel managed to give her a thumbs up sign before the helicopter door slid shut. Claire was sure it was the last time she would set eyes on him.

Three weeks later, she herself would be on a transport out of Baghdad. She was going back stateside, back to reality and hot showers and cable TV. Back to civilization and her work at the hospital. Claire smiled because she knew she was going home.

Chapter One

Three months later, Washington, D.C.

Claire sat up in bed quickly, ready to move. The sounds of gunfire and bombs echoed in her head, people shouting and the screams of the injured, the last remnants of a dream. Her breathing was labored as she tried to reorient herself to her surroundings. *You are home, you are safe!* Claire reassured herself. She kept repeating the words over and over in her mind while taking slow deep breaths.

The nightmares started a month after she got home. The first one was so bad she crouched on the floor in her bedroom for a half an hour, expecting the ground to shake from the weapons fire around her. It had taken time for her to realize she was not in Iraq anymore and she had been one of the ones who made it home okay. Every time she woke up from one of the nightmares, she had the smell of oil burning and the taste of dirt and blood in her throat.

She looked over at the clock on the bedside table, it said three in the early morning. Claire knew it was no use trying to go back to sleep. She would not be able to after the nightmare, so she got out of bed and padded into the kitchen. The hardwood floor was cool under her bare feet as she opened the door to the fridge.

She wished the damn nightmares would stop. They were less frequent, but hell, they were still cutting into her sleep. Claire didn't know why the nightmares started, she'd handled the fifteen months fine in country. She knew if she told anyone they would say post traumatic stress disorder, but she blew it off. She had been in the Army from the time she was eighteen. Thirteen years later, this was not her first time around the block. She moved up the ranks quickly to major, and when she had been deployed before, she came home right as rain each time. All she needed was to jump headfirst back into her routine and life.

She shrugged her shoulders and decided they would stop when they stopped.

She plopped down on the sofa and flicked on the TV. With a glass of milk in hand and a few Oreos, Claire watched reruns and then the morning news program until it was time for her to go into the hospital for her shift.

By six she was in her car driving to Walter Reed Hospital, where she worked. The automatic doors opened with a swoosh and Claire walked into the bright fluorescent lights of the ER.

"Morning, Dr. Kirkland, you're early." It was the voice of the head nurse, Sheila.

"Morning, Sheila, what have we got this morning?" Claire asked. "Was it busy last night?"

"Come on, Claire." Sheila laughed. "It's a full moon, you know all the crazies come out." Sheila had been working at the hospital five years as a nurse when Claire was transferred to the Medical Center, taking the position as the new ER head. Two years later they were still fast friends. Their friendship had formed almost instantly even when doctors in the hospital resented her getting the job. When she got her deployment papers Sheila was right next to her when she read them in her office. The other doctors figured she was more woman than a soldier, or even a doctor. She had proven them all wrong by showing them she could be both. No matter what had been said in the beginning, they could not say she did not do her job well. Claire was offered the job, bringing her to her hometown and closer to her mother. So she jumped at the chance.

Claire shrugged into her white coat and smiled. "Okay, I get it, but when I left last night I thought it was pretty slow. Are you leaving now?"

"Nope. I'm working a double, I'll leave at three. There's nothing on the board right now, Claire, but there is someone in your office to see you," Sheila informed her.

"Who?" Claire asked curiously. "I don't have any meetings with hospital heads today. We finished the quarterly budget last week."

"I don't know, some guy, very cute. Are you holding out on me?"

Claire laughed as she walked down the corridor to her office. "Shelia, you know I have the social life of a mole." Shelia's laughter followed her as she turned the corner.

"I can't cut anymore off the budget, Barry. You are going to have to live with it," Claire said firmly as she opened her office door. She looked up and stopped short. It was not Barry Moore, the head of the hospital, standing there. She was looking into the gorgeous green eyes of Sergeant First Class Daniel Butler.

Daniel smiled. "Sorry I'm not Barry, Major Kirkland."

"Uh…no, you are not, Sergeant Butler. And it's just Doctor Kirkland. I'm not in country anymore." No, he was definitely not Barry, the sixty-year-old head of the department. Claire felt her stomach do a few nervous flips before she quietly ordered it to stop in her head.

"How about I call you Claire? And since I am not in uniform right now, you call me Daniel," he said with a smile.

"Okay, Daniel, what are you doing in Washington and here in my office?" Claire asked. She walked in and stood behind her desk. Somehow she felt like she needed a barrier between them—he made her nervous but in an excited way. His presence seemed to dominate the small office, he was by no means a tall man, being just shy of six feet. But, his build was thick and muscular, his dark brown hair cut to military specifications made his features more bold. Claire took in the slightly crooked nose and the lips with the thin mustache. The whole package was quite appealing in Claire's opinion.

"Well, Claire," Daniel made a point to use her name and she couldn't help but smile, "I wanted to see you without a boonie hat on. I wanted to see if the angels that were swimming above my head when I got hurt were real. I am stationed out of the 69th Amory in Maryland, so it was no trouble getting here. And I wanted to thank you for saving my life."

"All that, huh?" she teased. "No thanks are necessary. I was doing my job and if it wasn't me, it would have been another medic." Why did his words make her work to breathe normally? The way he was staring at her made her feel warm on the inside.

Daniel took the few steps that took him to her desk. He reached over and took her hand, his voice low. "No, it was you, Claire. You said you would find me and you never did."

The touch of his hand sent a tingle though Claire's fingers, and she stammered on her next words. "You—you remember me saying that?"

"I remember lots of things. Like the color of your eyes. How did you get gray eyes like that, Claire?" His finger was tracing little circles on her wrist where her pulse beat, making the butterflies in her stomach do some new kind of dance.

"My-my father was Caucasian, my mom is African American." She laughed nervously. "Well, you can see one of my parents was black, since I am…."

"Your skin is like hot chocolate, I remember thinking that when I saw you at the party. I thought it again when the helicopter took me up," Daniel murmured, staring into her eyes. "You are stammering, Claire, do I make you nervous?"

"No," she said firmly. "No, you don't. And you can't come into a person's office, my office, and start touching them. I don't even know you."

"You do know me. Your pulse has picked up, so I am thinking you are telling me a fib."

Claire pulled her hand from his grasp and sat down behind her desk. "Well, my pulse is wrong unless you took up medicine since I saw you last."

Daniel laughed. "No, I didn't. So why didn't you find me, Claire, like you said you would?"

She stared at him in amazement. "You're kidding, right? How was I supposed to find you? I didn't even know where you were stationed, I said that to calm you."

"I took that comment very seriously. The first thing I did when I left Germany was to search for you, and I did find you."

"I don't know whether to be flattered or scared. Why would you want to find me?" Claire asked.

"Be flattered," he said with a smile. "I wanted to find you because."

"Because, that's the reason you have, just because?" At his smile and nod Claire added, "That's no answer."

"Well, come to dinner with me tonight and find out."

Just then Claire's beeper went off and she looked at it standing quickly. Before she could move her name was being paged over the speaker system. "I have to go, Daniel, I'm on call."

He grabbed her arm. "Tell me you'll come to dinner with me."

"Okay, I'll come to dinner. Pick me up out front around nine," Claire said without hesitation. She rushed out the door and she could still feel Daniel's gaze on her as she rounded the corner by her office.

* * * *

He strode out of the hospital into the bright morning sun and took a deep breath. He hated hospitals, and the inhaled breath took the smell of disinfectant from his nose. July in Washington was usually warmer than this, but today the humidity was nonexistent. Daniel walked between the passing people and took in the new day. He had parked his car a few blocks away and walked to the hospital. He was enjoying the freedom to walk, stretching his long legs, without worrying about what was coming.

For almost a year and a half in the desert, every step taken was careful and slow, not wanting to step on an IED or drive over one when they were on a mission. Improvised Explosive Devices, he had seen the damage they could do first hand. They demolished vehicles, and the human body was no match for the powerful homemade weapons. So now he could enjoy a walk, he would savor every step, until he went back.

Daniel's thoughts turned to Claire and a smile formed on his face. Claire Kirkland was a tough cookie, he could tell. But there was something under that tough exterior, and he wanted to find out what it was. She was wearing a short blue skirt and a matching blouse under the white doctor's coat. She had generous curves and hips, Daniel could imagine having his arms wrapped around her. A head full of thick, brown hair that was cut in the front with bangs—she probably got it cut when she came home, he mused to himself. A full, generous mouth completed her face, with those gray eyes that he could drown in. Claire

70

Kirkland had filled his mind when he was in Germany, and now he could not wait until tonight to have dinner with her.

Daniel's mind was so caught up in thinking about Claire, he was surprised when he was standing in front of his car. With a smile on his face, he slid behind the wheel and pulled into traffic. It was only a little after eight in the morning, and he did not have to pick her up until nine that night. Plenty of time to run his errands and get back to his place to change before picking her up for dinner.

* * * *

The call on her beeper was for a traffic accident that came into the ER. Two victims of a T-bone on the highway, and Walter Reed was the closest hospital *en route*. Claire worked in her usual efficient way—calming the woman who was more panicked than injured, and taking care of the man whose car took the brunt of the impact. He was sent up to X-ray for a broken collarbone and the woman was admitted for observation. While she was standing at the nurse's desk filling out charts Sheila came up to her.

"So, who was the stud in your office, Claire?" she asked curiously.

Claire laughed. "That was Sergeant Daniel Butler. I took care of him when he got hurt in Iraq a few months ago."

"He looks absolutely delicious. So, are you two going out?" Sheila probed.

"Well, Ms. Nosy, he is taking me out for dinner later as a thank you."

"Honey, if you saw how he looked at you when he was leaving. This dinner is not about a thank you," Sheila teased.

"Sheila, you and your romantic mind." Claire laughed, then she asked. "Did he look at me like that, like it's more than a thank you?"

"Claire, for a woman of thirty-one you are such an innocent. If Jeff looked at me like that I would not be coming in tomorrow," Sheila said speaking of her husband.

"You know that Jeff looks at you like that all the time. How many kids is it now? Three, including the new one I got pictures of overseas?" Claire teased in return.

Sheila hooted with laughter as she walked away with a patient's medicine. "I don't know how we do it, with our schedule. Even when we are together we are too tired for anything but sleep. I think the stork theory should come back into play."

Claire grinned at Sheila's comment, knowing that the plump woman probably had more of a sex life than she let on. *Daniel Butler*, Claire said the name in her head as she went back to her work. She was anticipating the night and what it could bring.

Chapter Two

By nine o' clock Claire was a bundle of nerves. What had made her say yes to Daniel's dinner proposal? She had walked into her office at eight-thirty to change. She thanked the heavens that she had the forethought to keep a few extra outfits in her office just in case. Amidst whistles and catcalls from teasing workers at her outfit, she walked through the sliding doors of the hospital and out into the fading light.

The sun had just gone down about an hour earlier. The night sky was a dark blue velvet blanket. Claire looked up as she stood outside. The sky was one of her favorite colors, and she was glad she was able to look up at it without wondering what was falling from it.

She was dressed in a light sundress the color of cream. On her feet she wore flat sandals and she had her hair falling loosely down her back pulled back to each side with a small crystal barrette. Claire loved to dress up lately since Iraq and only wearing a uniform day in and day out. She appreciated clothes in a new way, especially dresses and skirts.

She saw Daniel's smile as he drove up. He pulled up in front of her and leaned over to open the door to the sleek car. "Need a ride, pretty lady?"

Claire played along, feeling the light tone of his voice ease her nervousness. "Uh, I don't know, sir. I am waiting on my dinner companion."

"Drop that guy and come with me, I'm much better company," Daniel teased.

Claire tapped her chin as if considering the proposition. "Okay, he's out and you're in, buddy." Claire slid into the comfortable leather seat of the Saab and buckled herself in.

"You looked like a cool vanilla ice cream treat standing there in that dress," he commented.

Claire's laugh bubbled up naturally. "Your mind is on sweets, I see."

"No, it's actually on licking your skin to see if you taste as good as you look."

His words sent a curl of warmth through her belly that settled between her legs. What could she say to a comment like that? Hell, she wanted to see if he tasted as good as *he* looked, but she kept silent.

"Ready to go?" Daniel asked.

"As ready as I'll ever be."

Daniel pulled away from the curb and started down the busy street. He had the radio tuned to a nice jazz station. The music relaxing and mellow, Claire felt the day's tension begin to melt away.

Daniel glanced over at her and smiled. "So how was your day?"

"It went fine, honey, did you get the kids from soccer practice?" Claire teased.

"Hey, don't tempt me. I know a Commander who could marry us," Daniel replied with a grin.

I'm teasing, it's actually very nice to have someone ask me how my day was. And it was fine, by the way. Thank you for asking."

"Where would you like to go and eat?" Daniel asked.

"I'm not partial, but let's make it somewhere we can sit outside," Claire requested.

"I know just the place." Daniel turned the wheel and soon they were heading down Main Street. There was a comfortable silence between them. Claire was so relaxed she leaned her head back on the seat and closed her eyes. She must have dozed off because she felt a slight nudge to her shoulder. Her lids opened sleepily to see Daniel smiling at her.

Claire sat up right. "Oh my gosh! Did I doze off? I am so sorry, Daniel."

"You must have been more tired than you thought. I liked watching you sleep."

"You were watching me?" Claire asked. She leaned her head back against the seat.

"Yes I was. But if you don't move very soon I won't be able to stop myself from kissing you," Daniel said softly.

"Okay." It was a simple yes or no for her, everything inside her said yes to his kiss.

There was a smile on his face as his head descended to hers. His lips were soft and he moved them against hers lightly, just to enjoy the feel of her. Claire's lips opened under his, encouraging him to take the kiss deeper. Daniel did just that, his tongue invading her mouth swiftly. A low groan escaped him as her tongue followed back into his mouth. The kiss ended with Daniel pulling away, but not before he took one, two, three little tastes of her lips.

There was silence in the car, all they did was stare at each other before Daniel said. "Um, we should go in and….uh, eat."

"Yes we should, we came to eat, so we should go do that." Claire agreed with him.

Daniel got out of the car and walked around to open the door. He held his hand out to help her out of the car. She stood next to him and, still holding hands, they began to walk to the restaurant. There were lights twinkling from the trees out front. Each outdoor table had a candle floating in a bowl of water surrounded by flowers also floating in the water.

They were greeted at the door, and while they were waiting to be seated Daniel leaned over to whisper in her ear. "You know what?"

Claire smiled. "What?"

"That was some kiss," he said and kissed her softly on the ear.

Claire shivered and whispered, "I know."

Sitting outside in the warm night air, having dinner with someone, the soft music and romantic ambiance set the mood. Claire was having a good time and she forgot how good it felt just to relax. Daniel had ordered a bottle of wine and now they were talking as they waited for their food.

"So, how do you like being retired from the good old Army?" Daniel asked.

Claire took a sip of wine before answering. "It's kind of strange, but I like it. Who knew I could be a retired vet at thirty-one? How much longer do you have?"

"I don't get to retire just yet. I have at least one more tour before I can even put in my papers," Daniel replied.

"So you have to go back to Iraq?" Claire asked.

"In about two weeks. I have an eight-month tour coming up and then that's it."

"Oh." Claire's tone made him look at her curiously.

"Do I detect a note of disappointment in your voice, Claire?"

She smiled a shy smile. "I don't know, I guess after the kiss I figured we would have more time to get to know each other."

Daniel reached over the table and grasped her hand. "We can learn all we need to in two weeks. And I'll be back."

"I used to be a soldier too, Daniel," Claire said softly. "I know the risks and…"

Daniel stopped her. "Hey, I'll be back."

"Is it me, or does this seem to be moving very quickly? This is the first time we have seen each other since I treated you." Claire asked the question looking directly at him.

"Not fast enough to suit me," Daniel joked. "Seriously, Claire, this goes as fast or as slow as you want. But I have to let you know now. You have been in my thoughts all the way from the time I was put on that chopper, to when I saw you in your office this morning."

"I can't believe you even remember me, even though you were that hurt."

"I remember opening my eyes and looking at you. I remember you telling me you would find me. As soon as I was able to talk and ask who you were I started looking for you."

"I was meaning to ask you that. How did you find me?" Claire asked curiously.

"It was not easy," Daniel laughed. "First, after the surgery and I regained consciousness, I asked for the medic on the chopper. No one knew which chopper brought me in. So every time I heard a chopper I would ask to be wheeled out to the triage area to ask which one came in with me. I found him, then he gave me your name, and then it was just a matter of using my laptop to find you."

"You did all that to find me, why?" It amazed Claire that he would go through all that trouble.

"Yes I did, and as to why, because you captivated me with one look." His statement left her breathless in an instant.

"Do you go after things like this, so tenaciously?" she asked.

"Not things, Claire, you." Daniel looked at her as he spoke so she could see how serious he was.

Their dinner came, and Daniel changed the mood of their conversation. As they ate he found out her mom was a single mother and she joined the Army so she could go to med school. Claire found out that there was no one in Daniel's life. He was raised in foster care and, from the time he turned eighteen, the Army was his family. Claire felt sympathy for the lonely child who grew up without anyone.

She wanted to be that someone that he came home to. The thought startled Claire, where did it come from so suddenly, so quickly? Her gaze flew to Daniel's face and found him staring at her. She felt as if he was seeing her every thought.

"So, I guess I'd better take you home, huh?" Daniel asked conversationally. Dinner was over and they were chatting about any and everything, trying to prolong the good time they were having.

"Yes we should go. I have day shift all this week at work," Claire responded.

She gathered up her purse while Daniel paid the bill. On the walk back to the car they held hands, neither speaking, only enjoying the closeness that had quickly formed.

"Do you have to pick up your car from the hospital?" he asked as he opened the door of his car for her.

Claire slid into the car and looked up at him. "No, you can drop me off in the morning."

The door closed and Claire watched him walk around to the front of the car. Did she make the wrong choice? Claire was so sure she wanted to be with him tonight. His lack of response made her rethink her decision. *Maybe he didn't like such a bold offer, especially from a woman.* She knew most military men liked their women a little more submissive. Maybe it was because of her rank in the Army, that it was like an order instead of an offer. A lot of guys in the military had problems with women having a higher rank than them. Doubtful thoughts whirled around in Claire's head.

Daniel got in the car and started it up. Before he could change the gears to move, Claire put her hand over his on the steering wheel. "Did I say something wrong, should I not have assumed....?"

His response was to give her a hard kiss on her mouth. "No, I want to stay the night. I just want to make sure that you are sure."

"I'm sure, but you could have said something. I was thinking I should head for the hills or bury my head in embarrassment," she said. "I'm sure, Daniel, we have two weeks before you go. I want to enjoy every moment I can."

Claire laughed suddenly, making Daniel look over at her curiously. "What?"

"I cannot believe that I went from being nervous about dinner with you. To inviting you home with me. Here I was telling a friend this was just a thank you dinner from you," Claire explained.

"Claire, when I walked into your office, this was not about a thank you."

She looked at him. "I think I sort of knew that. By the way, I live on Florida Avenue in the Bloomingdale district."

"I know exactly where it is." He reached over and took her hand as they drove towards her apartment. It thrilled her to know that Daniel wanted her from the time he woke up in Germany. He was so sure that it was his intention to find her and make her his, this was some kind of man sitting next to her. Being a soldier, she knew that time waited for no one. That a minute, or even seconds, could make all the difference in life and in death. Daniel knew that as well. Doctor or soldier, the situation was the same. Time could be the changing factor in anyone's life. They were going to grab every second they could together and make it theirs.

Chapter Three

The drive to Claire's apartment seemed to take less time than usual, and soon they were standing in her living room. She was suddenly very nervous—Daniel's presence dominated her small space.

"Would you like something to drink?" she asked. She smoothed her hands down the front of her dress as if taking out unseen wrinkles.

Daniel noticed her gesture. "You don't have to be nervous, Claire. We don't have to do anything you don't want to do."

"I know. I'm just not accustomed to bringing men into my home, especially on the first date. I'm more of a long-term relationship kinda girl. In fact, my last boyfriend was before I left for Iraq and ..."

Daniel walked over and silenced her stream of words with his lips. He lifted his head to look at her. "No other men before me counts, and this is long term for me, okay?"

Claire nodded. He had managed to captivate her senses in only night, and she tried to clear her head before speaking. "I'll go get us some wine, or would you rather beer? I do keep some Michelob in the fridge."

"See, you were waiting for me, you have my favorite beer," Daniel said with a grin.

Claire smiled and went into the kitchen. A few minutes later, she came back with a glass of wine for her and a cold beer for him. He had made himself comfortable, she noted with a secret smile to herself. His shoes were off and next to her sofa and he was sitting with his legs crossed at the ankle, flipping through one of her photo albums. He looked at her and winked when she sat next to him and handed him his beer. The simple act sent a warm blush into Claire's face. God, she hated it when her body reacted this way. A seasoned soldier and she still blushed.

"Who is this with you sitting in a plastic wading pool?" Daniel asked.

Claire looked at the picture and laughed. "That's me and my sister Lucy. I think I was seven in that picture and she was nine. A hot Washington summer, no air conditioning, my mom pulled out the wading pool and the hose and we kept cool."

"Cute, look at you with all this hair in pigtails and wet," Daniel said. He looked over at her. "I like how you blush, Claire. It's very appealing."

"It's very bothersome," Claire replied, fanning her hot face. "I look like a cherry every time someone says anything in my direction. Imagine boot camp with this. The Sarge kept calling me Private Beets Kirkland for the six weeks I was there."

Daniel laughed out loud at that remark, and Claire swatted him with one of her soft pillows when he continued laughing. "Hey, it's not nice to laugh at your host."

"I'm sorry, "Beets," but I can't help it," he said, still laughing at her nickname. He tried to fend off the pillow coming at his head.

He caught the pillow and gave it a tug, pulling her along with it until she was sprawled across his chest. Claire was suddenly breathless as she was pressed against his muscled body. She could feel every contour of him through his thin shirt—the hard, sculpted body that the Army training had created. He pulled her head down to his for a long kiss. Claire opened her mouth willingly to accept his tongue and his taste. His hands roamed against her back, massaging her body and learning the feel of her. Claire made a little sound of pleasure in her throat as his hands moved to cup her breasts, slowly massaging the firm round globes. Her nipples hardened against his palms and Daniel groaned into her mouth. Their tongues mated and Claire pressed her body more intimately against his, trying to feel more of him. She had this need to be closer to his body and feel his skin against her own.

Daniel tore his mouth away from hers and looked into her eyes. "Yes?"

Claire knew the simple question was to give her the opportunity to back out and send him home. But she did not want to, she was sure about this night with him, more sure than she was about anything else in her life before now.

"Yes," Claire echoed his word. It could be nothing else but yes for her as she took his hand and led him to her bedroom. She walked over to the bedside table and turned on her lamp, the soft light filling the room. Claire watched his gaze roam her sanctuary, from the thick dark blue drapes she hung from the windows to the matching comforter on her bed. Then his eyes were on her again. She watched the heat smolder in them as her dress slipped from her body to the floor, and she stood in only a pair of black lace panties. Daniel walked over to her and slowly slipped his hand around her neck. Claire closed her eyes in pleasure from the sensation of his touch. She slipped her hands around his waist under his shirt, and in one fluid motion he pulled it over his head and let it fall to the floor. Claire pressed her face against his chest, feeling the soft hair against her cheek, and heard his heart beat speed up when she touched him.

"I want you, Claire," he whispered.

"You have me," Claire responded and she lifted her lips up to his for him to claim.

He kissed her as he swept her off her feet and laid her down on her bed. His gaze never left her as he slipped her panties off her smooth legs and then took off the rest of his clothes. Claire looked at his hard length as he stood proud and naked in front of her. On her knees, she pulled him closer until his legs bumped the mattress of the bed. She kissed the tip of his cock and took his length in her mouth, inch by slow inch. Daniel's breath hissed out between his teeth as Claire teased him with her lips and tongue. His fingers combed through and buried themselves in her hair, with every movement. She took his cock deeper into her mouth. With every sound that Daniel made in pleasure, it fueled Claire's own need.

Daniel pulled Claire away from him suddenly and kissed her hungrily, pressing her body back into the bed and covering her with his own. His lips traveled down to her breasts and he took the hard nipple in his mouth, moving from one to the other, hungrily tasting and suckling her. Claire cried out as ecstasy shot to her core. She bucked against him, wanting to feel him pressed inside her, but Daniel took his time in pleasing her. His hand traveled down her smooth stomach to the apex of her thighs. Then she felt his fingers slip between the moist folds of flesh and press against the secret bud that hid there. Claire could only press her hand against her mouth to smother her cries of passion.

"No." Daniel pulled her hand away. "I want to hear you come for me, don't hide it from me ever."

Claire closed her eyes as his fingers slipped inside her, his thumb pressed against her clit, rubbing gently. She felt his heated gaze watching as he sent her over the edge with his fingers alone. Claire felt her own body's release and how it flowed over his fingers. He did not let her catch her breath before she was filled with his thick cock.

"Daniel," she whispered breathlessly, wishing she could explain to him how good it felt to have him buried inside her. She could see none were needed as she looked at him. His eyes had gone dark with desire as he moved. Claire wrapped her legs around his waist and lifted her hips to take more of him. She felt his hand slip under her bottom to pull her into his every thrust. His breath harsh against her ear, she could hear him whispering his need, his words heightened her pleasure.

"Daniel...I'm going to come...please don't stop," she pleaded.

"No, baby, I'm not going to. God, you feel so good Claire. I can't hold back," Daniel moaned.

"You don't have to, come with me, lover. I want to feel you with me."

Claire felt his body tense and shudder against her as he pumped inside her. The sound of her slippery wet body meeting his filled the room.

"Daniel's fingers grabbed her hair." Look at me, Claire. I want to see you come, knowing it's me that's making you feel this way.

Claire opened her eyes as she spiraled into her orgasm. She watched Daniel's face as pleasure passed over it and his body tensed. His neck arched and a groan escaped his lips as he spilled himself inside her. With his head against her they waited for their bodies to stop shaking and their hearts to resume a normal rhythm. All the while she caressed his body, luxuriating in the feel of him and enjoying as he did the same to her.

"Maybe we should actually lay the right way in the bed," Daniel commented after a few moments.

Claire giggled. "Maybe we should since my legs are falling asleep hanging off the edge."

"You weren't complaining a few moments ago," Daniel replied as he kissed her neck.

"And I won't be later, either," Claire said with a sexy purr.

He looked at her. "So I get to stay the night? I was thinking you were going to kick me out after using my body."

"You get to stay the night, you nut."

"Good, because I wanted to fall asleep holding you," Daniel said softly.

Claire felt her heart warm with his words. "Good, because I wanted to fall asleep with you holding me."

They slipped under her midnight blue covers and he wrapped his arms around her. Claire knew that no one else could hold her like this, and for the rest of her life she would need to fall asleep in his arms.

Chapter Four

Claire turned her head on the pillow, her nose catching a whiff of coffee. She opened her eyes groggily and looked at the digital clock on her bedside table, it said six-thirty. She had slept, and for once the dreams that plagued her did not come. Slipping from the bed and finding her bathrobe, she walked through the living room to the kitchen. Daniel stood in front of her stove, stirring eggs in the frying pan. He wore no shoes, only his boxer shorts and her pink apron that said ARMY in bold letters over his bare chest. To Claire there could not be a more appealing sight.

"Well, don't you make a pretty picture?" Claire smiled as she leaned against the doorway of the kitchen.

"Hey don't knock the guy who is making you breakfast. Come over here and give me a kiss." He smacked his lips in her direction.

Claire laughed and walked over to give him a kiss. "Good morning, soldier, what's for chow?"

"Well, ma'am, we have eggs, coffee, and lightly buttered toast. How does that sound?

"Very nice, I could get used to this," Claire remarked.

"You'd better get used to it, lady, I plan to be doing it a lot."

"You'll be leaving in a week or two, Daniel…" Claire began…

"Until then I plan to spend every moment I can with you, and when I come home I'll be expecting to see you waiting for me."

Claire wrapped her arms around his waist and they stood there holding each other.

"Come on now, let's eat before it gets cold. I have to take you to work," he said softly.

"Okay, let's eat," Claire replied and she watched him walk away with two plates. She poured coffee for both of them and followed him into the other room.

They ate breakfast and talked. They took a shower together, which left Claire feeling breathless and weak in the knees. For the first time since she came home Claire arrived at work late. Daniel left her outside the hospital doors with a long, sexy kiss and a promise that he would meet her at her apartment when she got off work. Claire walked into the ER with a flush on her face that was not from the heat that had returned outside.

"Well, look at you, a half an hour late and a pep in your step," Sheila remarked as she walked in. She was getting her stuff to leave, her shift was over for the night. "Why, Doctor Kirkland, you look like you had a nice bowl of cream."

"Good morning, Sheila, how was your night?"

"Forget my night, how was yours?" Sheila teased. "And why do I think that blush is more that hot sergeant's fault than anything else."

"It could be," Claire said cheekily, "but my lips are sealed."

"Uh-huh, you are coming over very soon to dish about this, Claire." Sheila said. "But for now I am going to go home and try to catch a few minutes of alone time with my hubby and the baby."

"You do that, Sheila, sweet dreams."

Sheila waved a hand in farewell as she left, and Claire went into her office. The rest of the day was busy with the patients that came in and the everyday paperwork that came along with being head of the ER. It did not stop her thoughts from straying to Daniel. She could not wait to be in his arms once again.

* * * *

He watched her car pull up in front of her apartment hours later. Daniel leaned against his car with flowers in his hands, watching her get out and lean over to grab her bag from the back seat, leaving her sexy rump up in the air. Her smile made it all worthwhile, it was the look of a woman happy to see her man, and that was what he considered himself now, Claire's man.

"Well, this is something new, a hot guy waiting outside my door with a handful of flowers. Oh, what will the neighbors think?" Claire teased.

"Well, then let me give them something to really think about." He growled and pulled her into his arms.

His lips were on hers, kissing her deeply, submerging himself in her taste and in the feel of her body pressed against his. When he finally pulled away, her smoky gaze caught his. He saw desire in her eyes. His heart swelled because he knew there was no way that he could not come home to this, to have her look at him like that all the time. He ached as well, knowing that he would have to leave her soon.

"That is something to talk about, soldier. Let's go upstairs and discuss it in detail."

Daniel grabbed her hand and they walked the last few steps to her door. "No, no, you wench, you will not take me into your home and ravish me without food."

She laughed. "Oh fine, turn me on then leave me hanging. What do you want for dinner?"

"Luckily for you I thought ahead, pizza will be here in fifty minutes or so."

"Keep it up, you'll spoil me. I could get used to coming home after a long day of doctoring and find you waiting for me."

He turned and kissed her nose gently. "Get used to it, baby, get used to it."

The pizza went great with their conversation. Daniel played with her hair while they watched TV, letting his fingers graze against her scalp as he combed them though her thick locks. Her little purrs of pleasure at his touch fueled desire to his loins, and soon the television show was the last thing on his mind. He turned her face to him with the crook of one finger and teased her lips with a gentle kiss. It was a soft, feather light, sweet kiss filled with tenderness as well as passion. Daniel could feel his heart ache with a new kind of pain. It was going to be hell to let her go. Passion's flame took over from the tenderness and he submerged himself in her, letting his tongue sink deeply, searching for her taste. He moaned as her hand rubbed against his hard cock confined in his jeans.

Quickly he stripped off her shirt and let his tongue flick at her nipples that were already beaded into tight little buds. Claire arched her body more to his seeking mouth, silently begging him for more. Daniel let his hands run up her leg under her skirt to her ass before his caress glided over to cup her warm mound through the barrier of her lacy panties.

"Please touch me, Daniel," Claire pleaded softly.

When his fingers slipped between the scrap of cloth to rub her already wet clit, she cried out. He felt her body clench around his digit as he moved it deeper into her with every touch. He couldn't take it anymore, the need to feel her wrapped around his cock, to sink himself into her warm pussy was unbearable. While he freed himself from his pants, Claire slipped her panties off quickly and let her body straddle his. When she sank herself on his cock, Daniel arched his neck against the back of the sofa and luxuriated in the sensations assaulting his body from head to toe.

"I can't get enough of you, Claire. I will never be able to get enough of you," he whispered against her ear as he pumped his body inside her.

All words and thoughts were lost as they moved together. Her hips met his and ground down on his cock, and his lips sucked and teased her nipples. Soon their breathing changed as they strived for the ultimate completion that shook their bodies. Claire fell into the warm pools of her orgasm and Daniel soon followed with a moan that was mixed with the agony of having to leave her soon. *How am I going to live for the next few months without being able to feel her body next to mine?* His thoughts were soon erased for now when she began to trail soft kisses against his neck and their love dance began again.

* * * *

The next two weeks just flew by, it seemed to Claire. Daniel met her at the apartment every night after work— they had either gone out or stayed in and made love. They went picnicking on one of her days off. Relaxing next to the lake, they watched children play while the ducks swam in the water. They tried to fit as much as they possibly could into those two weeks.

It was on one of those nights, when he held her in her sleep, that the nightmare plaguing her came again. The noise of the mortars and gunfire filled her head, as did the need to take cover from sniper bullets seeming to be directed at her as she ran. Claire rolled off the bed to hide from the invisible entities chasing her in her dreams.

Daniel was up and next to her the second she moved off the bed.

As she yelled for him to get down before he got hit, he tried to calmly wake her up, speaking softly to her. "Claire, baby, it's a dream, you can wake up now. You are home and safe."

Claire came out of her dream with a startled shake. "Daniel? What? Where?"

When she figured out it was just a dream she gave a long sigh and got up and sat on the edge of the bed. "I'm sorry."

"What are you sorry about? It was a dream, how long have you been having them?" Daniel asked.

"Since I came home."

"You know its PTSD, right?"

"I know," she said in a resigned voice. "I just wanted it to go away on its own. I don't see why I am having it, I came home fine."

"That's why you have it, honey, it's called survivor's guilt, because a whole lot more didn't get to come home. Who did you lose in Iraq?" he asked softly.

Claire's breath caught. "One of my field medics. I sorta took him under my wing and he went out on his first mission, so cocky and grinning, giving me the thumbs up. When they came back in the next night, he was in a body bag. Blown apart by a Goddamn IED. Christ, he was only nineteen and he didn't even get to live."

"I know. I lost a few good friends over there and a few new ones as well. It's hard, but we have a duty and he knew. You can't be guilty for surviving, Claire, none of us can."

"I'm so scared you won't come back, Daniel," she whispered.

Daniel cupped her face in his hands. "I'm coming back because now I have someone to come back to."

"I'm glad you think so, 'cause if you don't I'm going to kick your ass," Claire said.

Daniel let out a bark of laughter and pulled her to him, tumbling them both on the bed. "Oh, you will, huh?" He tickled her and she squealed and wiggled. The dreams that woke her up were put aside for the moment as they played.

Chapter Five

The time past all too quickly, and soon it was their last night together. Daniel was leaving in the morning. Claire left work early and came home to make the night special for them. She made a romantic dinner and lit candles. She found the sexiest piece of lingerie she owned and when he knocked at her door she was ready.

When Daniel saw Claire standing there in a little red nightgown he was speechless. "Wow."

"I take it you approve of my attire," Claire said.

"Oh yes, I do. Claire you take my breath away," he replied and took her into his arms. "So, what is all this, hmmm?"

"I made you a special dinner. I figure for the next few months you'd be eating God awful Army food or MREs and I wanted to give you something good before you..." Claire's voice hitched as a sob escaped her lips."

Daniel tilted her head up to look into her eyes. "I'm going to come back, you know."

"I never knew it could be this hard. I have never been on this side of it. I don't want you to go, even though I know you have to," Claire whispered.

"I know, it's killing me to leave you, too." Daniel buried his face in her hair as he spoke.

Claire kissed him feverishly, holding him tightly. "We have tonight, we'll make it last as long as we can."

* * * *

Daniel kissed her in the same desperate manner, wanting to imprint her taste and how she felt in his arms. God, he was going to ache for her every day in that hot miserable desert until he could come home to her again. He lifted her against him and Claire wrapped her legs around his waist. Dinner was forgotten along with everything else for Daniel—all he wanted was to immerse himself in Claire. He walked with Claire until she was pressed against the wall next to the kitchen. Daniel's lips trailed down her neck to suckle her nipples through the silky material of her nightgown. He had this need to feast on her, and he intended to taste every part of her body before the night was over.

Her legs slipped to the ground and, even though their lips were fused, their hands tore at his clothes to free him of their confinement. Daniel went to his knees in front of her and slipped his hand under her thin nightgown. He tugged her tiny panties down her legs and his mouth was on her, tasting her womanly nectar. She tasted like sweet cream against his tongue as he slipped it between the soft folds of flesh. He felt Claire's hands on his shoulders and then his head caressing him as he tasted her.

"Daniel, Daniel," she chanted his name and spread her legs wider as he buried his face between them.

Daniel felt her body shake at the first tremors of her orgasm. As it overtook her completely with its force, her body flowed onto Daniel's lips and tongue. Daniel got up quickly and wrapped her legs around his waist, slipping his cock inside her deeply with one smooth stroke. With her back pressed against the wall he took her, thrusting into her deeply over and over again. Claire could only hold on in the storm he was creating.

"God, Claire, you feel so good. I don't know how I am going to live without you, without this, for so long," he muttered against her neck.

"Oh, Daniel," was all she could whisper as she held on to him. Even in the throes of their lovemaking their tears of sadness fell.

His body trembled along with hers as their passion reached the heights of ecstasy. He felt her body tighten around his manhood as she orgasmed on gasping breaths, and he groaned his pleasure as he felt his release over take him. Claire's legs fell weakly from around him and she laid her head against his shoulder. Daniel lifted her and walked on not so steady legs himself to the bedroom. He placed her in bed, climbing in next to her and pulling her close against him. Claire wrapped her arms around him, her tears on his skin, and Daniel felt his heart breaking. He had never had to experience this during his career in the military. He had been deployed, off to serve his country, many times before. He had watched as families said goodbye to their soldiers with tears from those who stayed and those who left. He always wished he had someone to tell him goodbye, and now that he did it felt like someone had stuck a shard of glass in his heart and twisted it cruelly so he could feel every bite of pain.

"Don't cry, baby, please don't cry." He tried to soothe her, but he felt his own tears clog his throat.

"I'm sorry, I really don't mean to cry. I wanted to send you off with a happy memory." She sobbed.

"I am the happiest I have ever been." He kissed her lips. "We have tonight, baby, the sun is still far way, we still have tonight."

They made love again in desperation, trying to keep the light of day away as long as they could. When the sun rose Claire drove Daniel from her place to the airport where he would be meeting the rest of his troop. Along with the rest of the wives, husbands and children, mothers and fathers, she said goodbye to Daniel. She watched as he walked away, he stopped, turned back, and pulled her into his embrace one more time.

"I love you, you hear me? I love you," he said fiercely and strode off quickly.

"I love you!" she yelled back though her tears. And he turned once more to beam a grin at her that could out shine the sun.

* * * *

Claire went to her mother's house straight from the airport and rang the doorbell.

Esther Kirkland opened the door. "Claire! This is a surprise, but why didn't you use your key?" She took one look at her daughter's face. "What the matter, what's wrong?

"I met this guy and I love him. He's a soldier and I just w-watched him walk away to get on a-a plane to go back to Iraq. Mom, I love him so much and I don't think I can handle this," Claire said and walked into her mother's arms sobbing.

Esther enfolded her daughter in a hug. "This was the first I'm hearing about this man that you love, baby."

"I know, Mom," Claire hiccuped. "I'll tell you all about him, I promise. We only had two weeks before he went back to Iraq. Right now I just need to hear you say everything will be okay."

"Oh, sweet girl, come on inside. It's going to be okay. He'll be fine, you'll see. I'll make us some iced tea and you'll get it all out, okay?"

Claire just nodded as she walked inside with her mother's arms around her. Thousands of miles above her, Daniel was sitting with the rest of his brigade going to the desert and missing his woman like crazy.

* * * *

The first few weeks for Claire went by in a haze. She went to work and did her job in her same efficient manner, but to her it felt like a part of her was missing. Her co-workers could see it but said nothing, except for Sheila. Claire had told her that Daniel had left to go back to Iraq, and she had even laughed a little when she told Sheila she loved him.

One day as Claire went through her shift at the hospital, Sheila stopped by her office to see her head down on her desk. "Hey, Claire, you want to grab some lunch?" Claire's head came up and Sheila saw the tears on her cheeks. She stepped in and closed the door behind her. "Aw, honey, are you okay?"

Claire nodded and wiped her face furiously. "I'm okay, I just get his face in my head and I miss him and I can't stop the tears."

"That's love, honey. If my man had to be in that position, I would have to join up, too. I couldn't handle it without him. It makes me appreciate him being home when I get there. It will be fine, he'll be home soon," Sheila said, comfortingly rubbing her shoulder.

Claire sniffed. "I know."

"So, you wanna go to lunch, my treat?" Sheila asked hopefully.

"Not today, I feel tired and achy. I think I am coming down with the flu," Claire replied.

"Well, if you are sick, I'm sure one of the on-calls would cover for you to go home."

"No, I want to work as much as possible. I can't sit at home and think, I need to keep busy."

Claire's days and nights were filled with thoughts of Daniel. She knew the routine, it would take awhile for him to get to Iraq, and then a convoy trip to where he and his battalion would be based. Claire knew the operating bases were long distances in between, with rough desert and insurgent groups. So until he got to his base she would not receive a phone call. She would work and keep busy until he came home.

She worked her shift and a few hours overtime so she could be tired and just fall into bed to sleep. She really did think she was coming down with something because she felt completely exhausted when she got home that night, more than usual after a long shift. She kicked off her shoes and clothes and sat in front of her laptop to check her mail before she went to bed. Her screen flashed on and she clicked quickly to skim though her e-mails until she came to the e-mail address that was named *Clairesguy38@yahoo.com*. Her heart leapt in her throat and her hands shook as she clicked to open the email and read...

My dearest Claire:

We haven't gotten to base yet. We stopped at one of the outposts for a day and they happened to have a computer link. I bribed one of the guys to let me get on it really quickly to create this e-mail account and to e-mail you. This is your special e-mail address, e-mail me here as much as you want and I'll reply as much as I can. I'll call you as much as I can too, every day when we get to the base and there are no sandstorms (you know how they are). Guess what, I bought a webcam in Germany so you can see me when I get to use Yahoo Messenger. Can you get one too so I can see you? Take pictures and send them to my e-mail. I need to see your face as much as I can to get through these months. (Naughty pictures will be appreciated). It's damnably hot here! I keep picturing myself with you in your bed eating the strawberry ice cream you like so much. I liked especially that I got to lick it off your belly. Gosh, I miss you so much, Claire. I see your face every time I close my eyes. A little secret (Uh, I borrowed a pair of your undies from your drawer when I was leaving).

Claire laughed out loud as she read that piece of the letter, then continued reading:

I'll bring them back, I promise. I need something that smells just like you to keep me going over here. I have to go now, the guy I bribed is giving me the look. Baby, I miss you so much and I love you, I swear I love you now and always. Kisses to you, my love.

Daniel...

PS... I have had so many dirty dreams about you since I left. I wrote one out for you. I'm not really good at story telling but here it goes...

I love the smell of your hair as I'm holding you in my arms, standing behind you. You pull your hair over to one side exposing your neck and tender earlobe.

You feel the heat of my breath on your skin as I slowly kiss your neck, and begin to rub my hands from your waist up to your breast. I can feel your nipples begin to harden under your shirt. You begin to breathe deeper as I start to suck on your ear and begin to unbutton your shirt. You reach to hold my head as I continue to lick your neck and ear. You can feel my cock grow hard as your ass is pressed up against me. I slide my hand under your bra and rub my fingers across your hard nipples and begin to gently squeeze both, at the same time you reach behind to feel my hard cock as it bulges from my pants... You start to purr, as I slide my hands down your stomach to undo your pants, sliding one hand down between your legs, and feeling the warmth and wetness of your pussy. You pull my hand up and slowly lick my fingers tasting your sweetness.

I continue to slide your pants to your ankles and you step out of your pants, turning toward me on your knees you begin to unzip my pants and pull them quickly off for you can't wait to get my cock in your mouth.

You begin to suck my cock, licking the shaft and taking special attention to run your tongue up from the bottom, to the tip before you suck the head of my cock. You can feel my cock pulse as you suck it. You squeeze the head as you suck my balls, don't stop, you are doing great. You continue to suck my dick, taking it all the way in down to the base. "I love how you taste me" You keep that up and I will explode in your mouth. I have to stop you; it feels so good it is almost unbearable.

I grab and lift you up, carrying you to the bed. There you lay, waiting for me as I move in between your legs spreading them apart. My cock hard and ready, I slowly ease it into your wet and swollen pussy lips, you begin to moan again as I slowly begin to stroke it in and out. You begin to move your hips with me and we begin our dance of loving each other. I feel your pussy get hotter and wetter each time I stroke you. You tell to me fuck you harder, "pound me hard baby—make me cum" I lift your legs up on my shoulders. And begin to long stroke you, my balls smacking your ass each time I drive my cock in deeper and harder. You squeeze your nipples for me as I watch. You are dripping wet and I continue to fuck you hard. You reach and grab my ass cheeks and feel my balls smack your little brown love button each time.

Claire read and reread that e-mail over and over again. She had to fan herself while she read before she typed her own e-mail to Daniel. Her heart felt so full, relieved because he was okay and she finally had heard from him. The heat at the end of his letter left her body aching and made her quiver. Daniel had succeeded in making her hot and wet with his words. *Not a good story teller, my ass,* she thought as she wrote. She was filled with love like she never felt before. They would be okay and he would be home to her soon.

She finished her e-mail, turned off her computer, and went to bed, and for the first time since he left she slept until morning and without the bad dreams.

* * * *

Daniel walked into his trailer, tired and hot and miserable. He had spent so long trying to get to the Operations Base that he had sand in places he did not care to think about. He took a sniff of himself and wrinkled his nose, making a mental note that a bath was his first priority.

He dropped his heavy pack on the floor of his new home for the next eight months. It was nothing more than a big truck container with windows and a small air conditioning unit that did little to cool the hot air. Shelves made of plywood would hold his stuff, the things he did not take with him when he was out on missions. He was based out of Camp Regan this time—his mind went back to the camp where he had first met Claire and his heart ached for her. He took up his things to go and take a shower, and instead of walking to where the men took their showers he walked to the recreation center where the soldiers could make phone calls and use the computer.

He would not be able to call her yet. They had just arrived and did not have the proper authorizations in place. But, he would be able check and see if she had e-mailed him. His few minutes turned into a half an hour wait to use a computer. He was in the company of other guys who stunk to high heaven, so Daniel did not feel too badly about his own smell.

Finally he got to click on his e-mail and he saw one from *DanielsHeart30@yahoo.com.* Even though it was from a week before it was the greatest thing he ever saw. He had no one to e-mail him or even talk to back home before, but now he had her. A smile broke his face as he began to read.

Daniel,

I was so worried until you e-mailed me. It's getting cooler here in Washington and you know right after Labor Day the leaves will change and we will be in autumn. I wish you could be here with me to see the leaves change and walk with me. I told my mom about you, well, I cried about you right after you left. You have been summoned to her house for dinner as soon as you get home (smile). Don't worry, she is harmless, she won't bite. I hope you get to your FOB soon, I hate thinking about you out there without any cover. You have to promise me that even when it gets bad you will tell me and not try to sugarcoat it. I was a soldier, too, after all and I want you to be able to lean on me. I will buy that webcam after work tomorrow so when you get to base you'll be able to see me. As you can see I created your own special e-mail as well. I will not be outdone and I need it to use the webcam. I'll have a few naughty pictures for you by the time you contact me again. How does a pink lace teddy sound? By the way, you stole my favorite pair of red panties when you left. I expect them back minus the sand.

Daniel laughed out loud when he read that part of her e-mail. Other soldiers looked around at him and he quieted down to finish reading his e-mail from his woman.

I know what you mean about the missing my love, because I feel like I have this great big hole in my life and it will only go away when you come home. I love you, too,

Daniel so very much with all my heart and soul. I have to go to bed now, panda bear. It was a long day at the hospital and I feel kinda like I am catching the flu. I'll be fine, don't you worry about me. You keep your head down and be safe, my darling man. I love you always.

Claire...

PS. I hope you know you almost made me orgasm just by writing that little note to me. I want everything you described when you come home. As you close your eyes tonight, I want you to picture me over you, straddling your hard body and riding your cock. Picture holding me close and kissing me while I make love to you. Feel my love surround you and keeping you safe...

Daniel started to type on the key of the computer in front of him. Soon he was done, but he did not want to move from the computer. It was the only connection he had to her, until the person next in line cleared his throat to let him know other people were waiting. Only then did Daniel move to go take his long-awaited shower and to get something to eat. He would picture her tonight doing all she said and more. His Claire missed him and would be waiting for him to come home.

* * * *

Two weeks later, Claire sat in her office, stunned. Sheila stood in front of her desk, looking at her and grinning broadly.

"You are sure about this, Sheila? Absolutely positive?" Claire asked.

It was the third time she had asked the question, and Sheila simply said. "Yup."

"You could stop grinning like a loon, Sheila," Claire said. "And you are positively sure?"

104

"I am three hundred percent sure, honey. You are pregnant!" Sheila squealed.

"Uh-huh."

"Aren't you excited?" Sheila asked.

"I don't know what I am," Claire murmured. "But you seem excited enough for both of us."

Claire had spent the three weeks after her first e-mail with Daniel feeling achy and miserable. They had exchanged e-mails every day since then, but she still had not heard his voice. His base was in the middle of sandstorms and bad weather, plus a couple of insurgent attacks. The combination of all those things had made communication to the States impossible. When she woke up with her first taste of nausea Claire started to think it was something other than the flu. She had Sheila run a blood test, and now she stood in front of her confirming her suspicions.

"So when can you give Daniel the good news?' Sheila asked excitedly.

"Is it good news? We never talked about kids, Sheila!" Claire cried, standing up suddenly and pacing the room. "We never got to talk about anything! We had two weeks before he left, he has barely been gone two months and then I say, hey guess what, I'm pregnant! How is he going to take that!?"

"He loves you and he will be thrilled," Sheila said firmly. "He'd better be or when he gets back here I'm going to kick his butt back to Iraq."

Claire was hardly listening as she paced. "How will I tell him? How will I tell my mother!" She whirled and grabbed Sheila by the shoulders. "My mom is going to kill me!"

Sheila laughed out loud. "How old are you? Claire, you are almost thirty-two years old. Your mom cannot kill you, she will probably be happy to have a grandchild on the way."

Claire said in a dazed voice, "Yeah, you are probably right."

So when are you going to tell him?"

"I'll e-mail him tonight, and wait for a reply, a good one I hope."

"It will be." Sheila assured her.

Claire wondered if it would be good news. Daniel was the first man she loved in such a long time, and she never loved anyone like she loved him. Would it be ruined now because of an unwanted pregnancy? By him at least— Claire already knew in her heart from the time Sheila said she was pregnant that she wanted the life growing inside her. She only hoped that Daniel would share in her joy.

Later that night she went to her mother's house and told her the news. Her mother's tears of joy made her happy, and when she got home she sat in front of her laptop and did not know how she should put it in an e-mail to Daniel. It was not like sending naughty, suggestive e-mails and sexy pictures. This was important, and finally she began to type.

Darling Daniel;

I miss you and love you madly. I have something to tell you and I hope you are happy...
And baby makes three? What do you think?

Claire...

She turned off her computer and sat on her bed. All she could do now is wait and hope for the best. *God, now I am nervous and I want ice cream*, she thought to herself. She smiled as she walked to her kitchen and opened the freezer. Pregnancy would at least let her give into the craving for junk food she tried to abstain from. It would not be so bad being pregnant alone, she decided. Her mom would be there, and until Daniel came home she would have to be strong for her and the baby. It would be fine, he would be happy, she assured herself, but the doubts about how this news would affect him still wavered in the back of her mind.

Chapter Six

Daniel spent a week out in the desert leading a mission. He was tired, hot, and missing Claire like crazy. He had not been able to check e-mails before he left, and he did not even know if they had a phone line to the States as yet. He dreamed of Claire and all the sexy poses she had sent him via e-mail. He woke up with a hard-on every morning and he felt his cock grow now as he thought about her.

More than six months left before he could touch her again. She'd be lucky if he got out of the airport without making love to her when he got home.

He dropped his dusty pack on the floor of his trailer and walked over to the recreation area. Check e-mails first, and then shower and eat. A few e-mails from Claire seemed more important than a shower and a hot meal at that point.

He passed a soldier coming out of the recreation area. The young man instantly saluted as Daniel walked up. "Hey, soldier, do you know if the phones are up?"

"Sir, they are up and working, sir!"

"Thank you," Daniel replied and saluted.

He walked in thinking he would check his e-mails first and if a phone were free then he would call. There was little to no one in the room because when he came it was daytime and everyone was off doing their duties for the day. But when he looked at the phones they were all in use. *At least the computers are free*, he thought as he sat down tiredly and typed in his screen name and password. He saw Claire's e-mail there, only one in the last week, he mused. *Maybe she got busy at the hospital*, he thought as he clicked to open the message.

He read the message and his mouth fell open—he read it again and again. He moved so quickly that his chair toppled over, and rushed to the phones where there was people still waiting.

"I need to use a phone now!" he shouted.

One of the commanders of the unit came out of his office. "Is there a problem, SFC Butler? Your rank does not mean you get privileges above the other soldiers when it comes to calls."

Daniel instantly stood at attention. "I understand, sir, but I was gone for a week and I just got some news that I have to call home immediately, sir. I'm going to be a dad and I couldn't call......."

The commander held up his hand, cutting off Daniel's stream of excited words. Daniel knew it was an unusual site for the commander. He could never say he had ever seen his sergeant this excited in the years he had known him, and for good reason. "Come into my office and we'll get you a line out. I think news like this deserves a little rule bending."

Daniel stood excitedly as his commander worked on getting him authorization for a call. He handed Daniel the phone and left him alone in his office for privacy.

To Daniel it seemed like the phone rang endlessly until Claire picked it up.

"Hello?" Her voice was groggy and filled with sleep.

"Claire, it's me, baby!" he said. "We're pregnant!"

"Daniel?" she said. "I sent you an e-mail a week ago."

"I know, baby, I'm sorry. I was on a mission and I didn't get to check my e-mails before I left. Is it true are you going to have a baby?"

"I thought you read it and didn't want me anymore," she said quietly.

"Don't you dare think that! I know I woke you, I'm sorry, but I had to talk to you. I haven't since I left," he said.

"It's after two in the morning here, and yes you are going to be a dad," Claire said. "How do you feel about that?"

"How do I feel? I love it!" Daniel shouted. "Damn, me a dad, how far along are you?"

"About eight weeks give or take, summer delivery date," Claire replied. "By the time you come home, you'll be a daddy."

"I miss you, Claire, you sound so good. It feels like forever since I heard your voice. And this is the most wonderful news I could ever have."

"Daniel, I miss you too so much. I wish you were here," she whispered. "I'm kind of scared to go through this by myself. But I have my mom and Sheila, who said she would be my birth coach."

"Honey, I wish I was there to go through every little step with you," Daniel said in a longing voice. He really wanted to see his child grow in her tummy and watch her bloom with motherhood. He had been alone in the world for so long. Now, he had a family. It seemed like a dream, and he did not want to wake up if it was.

"Honey, I'm on my commander's line and I can't stay any longer. I'll call you when I can, I promise. And I'll e-mail," he said hastily.

"Okay, I'm glad you are happy, Daniel. I love you," Claire said with tears in her voice.

"Oh, honey, don't cry. I love you, too, both of you," he said softly.

"It's the hormones," she said mistily. "It happens to pregnant women, you know."

"Bye, sweetheart," he said with a small laugh and he hung up after he heard her goodbye.

Daniel walked out of his commander's office with a big grin on his face. He barely felt the slaps of congratulations on his shoulders. He was going to be a father, the thought amazed him as he showered and ate. He lay in his bed looking at her picture that he had printed off the computer and hung in his trailer. Claire had his child growing inside her. The time he had left serving his tour seemed unbearable now.

* * * *

Claire tried to make him feel as included as she possibly could in the life growing inside her. It was so hard for him, she knew, not to be there. So in every e-mail she tried to tell him about what was going on and included pictures of her expanding waistline. She sent him a care package filled with little treats from home and it included a tape of their baby's heartbeat. Every e-mail and every call from Daniel was filled with sweet words of affection, how beautiful he thought she was, and how he could not wait to come home to her and the baby.

There were sandstorms. He went out on missions. During that time there were no calls or e-mails from him. She would sit and worry even though she knew exactly why he could not reach out to her. It did not make it any easier; in fact, it made it worse because she had treated many soldiers for injuries after they came back from being on a mission.

The seasons had turned from fall to winter in D.C. The time was spent with her missing Daniel, work, and watching the life grow inside her. She was five and a half months into her pregnancy and Sheila already accused her of waddling while she was at work. She was so happy she had Sheila. She was a godsend, keeping Claire sane and was there when the crying jags started. She went with her to every doctor's appointment, and her mother went as well. She made sure Claire had dinner with her at least twice a week so Claire was eating okay. She knew her mom worried about her being alone, so she let her dote and fuss all she wanted.

She sat in her office after her shift and read of one his e-mails. Claire had sent him an e-mail earlier that day after her doctor's appointment and included the first sonogram pictures of their child. She hadn't expected an e-mail back from him so soon, but on a whim decided to check and found he had replied soon after she had sent it. There were points where the loneliness felt unbearable to her and she so badly wanted to feel his arms around her. This was one of those times as she read his words.

Darling Claire:

How are you, my love? I bet my kid is kicking up a storm, huh? I got the sonogram picture, thank you for marking where the baby is outlined. I have never even seen a sonogram so I could not tell you what I was looking at. It all just looked like a bunch of squiggles to me. You are the doctor, so I'll leave all that to you. I loved looking at it, that is my child in there and I have never felt like I have been given more of a gift than I do now. Is it a boy or a girl? No, don't e-mail it to me, tell me when I call you later. This is news I want to hear from your lips. Those sweet delectable lips that I miss kissing. I wish I was there to put my hand on your stomach and feel him or her move.

We have had a lull here, it's been quiet, so we have been able to take a few days of really good rest. But as you know this does not last long, so everyone is trying to enjoy it as best we can for as long as we can. I can't wait to come home to you. When I come home we'll go house hunting, that way the baby can have his or her own room and a backyard. I want to give everything that I never had to the baby, a home and a family, a backyard where they can play. I longed for those things when I was growing up, jumping from foster home to foster home. I figured out after meeting and loving you that I still longed for those things. I just put them in the back of my head. Now you have given me both to look forward to when I get home.

I love you.

Daniel

After Claire read the e-mail from Daniel she got up to go home. The ER was still abuzz as she walked out into the cold night in Washington. She slid behind the wheel of her car and drove slowly through the streets that were still lightly dusted from the snowfall from the night before. February in Washington was bitterly cold. As she drove Claire felt the tiny life inside her wiggle and squirm. A smile crossed her lips and she gave her tight stomach a little rub. She would go home and have dinner so the little one would relax and wait for Daniel's call.

Chapter Seven

"Damn!" Daniel muttered. This was the second time he had called Claire's phone and there was no answer. He called her cell phone as well and it went to her voice mail. He was just about to hang up again when he heard her soft voice on the phone.

"Hello?"

"Claire, are you okay, is something wrong?" Daniel asked in a panicked voice. "I called and you didn't pick up, I was about to call your mom."

"No, I'm fine, honey. I fell asleep and I sleep like the dead lately." Claire's voice was husky with sleep and to Daniel it was sexy as hell. "Why would you call my mom?"

"Because I couldn't reach you, and I thought the worst."

"I should have never given you her number for emergencies, you are just as bad as her with the worrying," Claire grumbled. "If you had called her, I would have heard her screeching up outside my place and kicking my door in."

Daniel laughed, picturing it in his head. "Your mom is not that bad, Claire."

"Wait until you meet her. How are you, Daniel, I mean really?" Claire asked softly.

He sighed. "I'm good, baby. We had a few injuries come into the FOB from a mission that went out, but like I said in my e-mail, it's been quiet. Now give me my news, who's going to be calling me daddy? A boy or a girl?"

"Maybe I shouldn't tell you," Claire teased. "Maybe I should make you wait until you get home and we meet you at the airport."

"You could not be that cruel, my love."

Claire laughed. "To you, no I couldn't be. You are the father of a little boy, Sergeant Butler."

Daniel whooped with joy and yelled, "I'm having a boy!"

"Hey congrats, Sergeant B.!" someone called out from behind him.

"Ugly baby if it looks like you, hope he gets Mom's looks," another commander teased.

"Do you hear these guys?" Daniel laughed.

"Yes I do. Tell them you are the most handsome man there," Claire replied. "I take it you approve?"

"Hell yeah, that's my boy in there!" he replied. "Put the phone to your belly so I can talk to him."

Claire did as he requested and then said, "Okay, you can talk." She smiled as she heard him saying something to her belly but could not understand what he was saying.

"So what are we going to name this little guy?" Daniel asked Claire.

"I was thinking he would be Junior," Claire said but added hastily, "But if you don't want to, it's okay. I can give him my last name."

"Why would you think that, seems a little strange that he'd be Kirkland and his mom and dad are Butlers," Daniel replied. "I thought you knew as soon as I get home we are getting married."

"Really? It would have been nice to be asked, you know," Claire shot back. "Besides, who says I want to marry you?"

Daniel's heart dropped. "You don't want to marry me?"

"I didn't say that. I just would like to be asked instead of you assuming that this is how it's going to be."

"Major Claire Kirkland…." he began to say.

"Retired," she interrupted.

"Retired Major Claire Kirkland, would you do me the extreme honor of becoming my wife?"

"Hmmm, let me think," Claire said with a smile in her voice.

"Claire," he warned.

"My answer is yes, Daniel, there is no one I would want to spend my life with but you."

"Good, 'cause I feel the same way. I gotta go, baby, my time is up on the phone. I love you and will talk to you soon," Daniel said.

"Bye, honey, I love you, too."

* * * *

Claire was in her final weeks of pregnancy. It was the middle of June, and in about two weeks she was going to deliver her first child. She was on maternity leave from the hospital and was at home trying to rest. Only she could not rest, it was a month since she had heard from Daniel. She was gripped with fear every day that passed when she did not hear from him. Was he somewhere injured? In a hospital, in a coma? He was listed as no family even though when he left he updated his information. She was supposed to be contacted in case anything happened to him. Claire knew that sometimes records got lost, and even if it was updated here in the States, it could not be overseas. He could be lying somewhere unable to tell them anything. Even worse, he could be dead.

Claire's worry affected her health in the final stages, her blood pressure kept spiking. Her doctor wanted to put her in the hospital to monitor her, but Claire refused to go, not wanting to miss his call. So instead her mother was with her round the clock, and Sheila spent as much time at her apartment as she possibly could. They both watched as Claire worried, and tried to comfort her as much as possible. Today they were both at the apartment.

"Claire, you have to sit and rest," Esther Kirkland said, looking at her daughter.

"I'm fine, Mom," Claire replied.

"No, you are not, your blood pressure is hovering on the brink of dangerous," Sheila piped in.

"I'm a doctor, Sheila, I know my own body," Claire snapped and then sighed. "I'm sorry, Sheila, I don't mean to snap at you, it's already so hot and…"

Her mother stood and held her by the shoulders. "And you are worried about Daniel. He is fine, Claire. You used to be there, you know how communication is."

"But never this long. He told me he would call the next day, Mom, and that was four weeks ago! He might be hurt or…"

"Don't think like that, Claire! What about when you called your friends in the military? What did they say?" Sheila asked.

"They can't tell me anything, where he is, if he is on mission, no one knows!"

"Calm down," her mother soothed and looked at Sheila with a worried expression.

"You need to go lie down, right now," Sheila said firmly and steered her towards the bedroom.

Claire looked around to where she had set up the bassinet for the baby and hung a mobile with blue stars and airplanes. She had put a few things on the wall and even set up a changing table and rocking chair. Her one-bedroom apartment would be home until Daniel returned and they could find a house. She felt tears sting her eyes as she thought that maybe he would not get to see the tiny things she had done to welcome the baby. He might not even get to meet his son or sit in the rocking chair and hold him.

She could feel the tiredness in her body, and as she got into bed she asked Sheila. "Do you think he is okay?"

"He is fine, absolutely fine, but he would want you to rest and take care of his son and be well when he comes home," Sheila replied softly.

"I know, I am tired," she admitted as her head rested against the pillows on her bed.

"Then go to sleep, we can have dinner when you wake up." Sheila encouraged.

* * * *

Sheila walked back into the living room after getting Claire settled.

Esther Kirkland sat with her hands folded in her lap, and looked up at Sheila. "Is she asleep?

"Getting there, she was tired," Sheila said.

"I wish Daniel would call, she has always been so strong and I have never seen her like this. I don't think she will be able to handle it if something has happened to him."

"Nothing has happened to him," Sheila said firmly. "And if the worst happens we will be here to help her through it all."

Esther nodded and got up. "I'll get some dinner started so when she wakes up she can eat. She has to keep her strength up."

"I'll help."

The women walked into the kitchen, both worried about Claire and Daniel. Making dinner was the only way they could think of at that moment to keep busy, while praying in their own minds.

* * * *

Their collective prayers were answered four days later. Claire's mother had gone home to take care of some errands before coming back to Claire's apartment. Sheila had stopped by after work and now was sitting on Claire's sofa while Claire was in the kitchen getting her favorite pregnancy comfort food of late: black cherry ice cream with canned fruit cocktail with heavy syrup over the top and tons of nuts. Her worry had been non-stop, but she was trying to keep calm so as to keep her pregnancy healthy.

"I don't know why you don't let me get that for you," Sheila called out.

"You don't do it right," Claire responded. "I like it done a certain way. Do you want one?"

"No thanks, unless you want me in a sugar coma on your chair."

"There was a knock on the door and Claire made a detour from going to the living room to answer it." Mom, why do you always knock when you have a key, plus it is un…?"

Claire's words stopped mid-sentence, the bowl of ice cream that she had made fell from fingers that had suddenly gone numb, smashing onto the floor. She was looking into the green eyes of Daniel who stood in his uniform at the door. Sheila rushed around the corner to see them standing there looking at each other.

"Hi, my love," Daniel said softly taking in her face and her very swollen belly.

Tears were streaming down her face as she looked at him. She reached up a trembling hand to touch his face, she had to make sure he was real. When her fingers touched his skin he pulled her into his arms. Her sobs filled the air and he buried his face into her hair, inhaling her scent with closed eyes.

"I-I thought you were gone, no one would tell me anything! I was s-s-so worried." She tried talking through her tears. "Why didn't you call? Why?"

"I'm so sorry, honey." He pulled away kissing her lips and face and eyes tasting her tears. "I got called out on a mission and we just had to leave. By the time we got back our time was up. We lost some guys in an ambush on our last mission. They sent us straight back out with the convoy to go home, then a two-week stay over in Germany."

* * * *

It felt so good to hold her, after all those months away from her it felt like heaven to him. He felt movement against him when the life inside her stirred. He was home at last and he could feel his own tears fill his eyes.

"Because of the deaths we were not allowed to make calls or use the Internet. At that point I just wanted to get home to you. We got a flight out yesterday. No one knew we were coming, baby."

He could tell Claire was only half listening as he recounted his tale. She was busy running her hands over his face and neck and back and staring into his eyes. Her love shined through the tears and she kissed him fiercely to show him how much she missed him. Daniel felt her stiffen against him and pull away with a surprised look on her face.

"Claire, what's the matter, baby, what's wrong?" he asked.

"I-I think my water just broke," she whispered, looking down as a puddle formed at her feet. "Sheila!"

Sheila came running around the corner and looked from Claire to Daniel with a grin on her face. "Looks like this is some homecoming! You got here just in time, big boy!" she said, slapping him on the back. "Call Claire's

120

mother and tell her to meet us at the hospital. We are going to get her cleaned up and get on the way."

Daniel stared after them, watching Sheila help Claire to the bedroom and close the door. A huge smile spread across his face and he rushed to the phone that hung on the kitchen wall. Dialing the number, he waited until he heard her mother pick up. "Hi, Mom, I'm home and we are having a baby!"

Esther's scream of excitement came across loud and clear on the phone and Daniel grinned. Sheila was right this was some homecoming.

Chapter Eight

Daniel and Sheila helped Claire into the back seat of her car and Sheila slid behind the wheel to drive. Daniel got in next to her and tried to soothe her through the contractions that had begun soon after her water broke.

Seeing her in pain, Daniel asked, "You are getting some sort of medication for pain at the hospital, aren't you?"

"It's called an epidural, and no I am not. I decided to do this the natural way. Oh, here comes another one!" she gasped out and leaned her head back against the seat of the car and started her slow breathing.

"Are you timing these contractions, Daniel?" Sheila asked.

"What? No, I was supposed to? Crap!" he said in a panicked voice. "Sheila, you're a nurse, shouldn't she have something for the pain, it will get worse, right?"

"Don't panic, Daniel, she can have it if she wants it, now time those contractions and calm down," Sheila said with a smile. "I think that she should have it too, but hey, I'm just the coach."

"Hello, I am a doctor, did you forget that?" Claire snapped. "Quit talking like I am not here. I can do this without damn drugs!"

"Hormones," Sheila explained to Daniel who nodded in understanding.

"Any more contractions?" Daniel asked, worried. He was as excited as was humanly possible at the impending birth of his son, but scared when he saw her in pain. This was his Claire, and if anything happened to her it would be his fault.

"If I was having one you would know, trust me." Claire began to cry. "I'm sorry for snapping at you! You just came home and here I am biting your head off. I missed you so much and I love you!" she wailed.

"It's okay, baby, you yell at me as much as you want. I'm a soldier, I can take it." Daniel wrapped his arms around her as she sobbed. He shot a helpless look at Sheila, who was watching the scene from the rear view mirror. He could deal with men shooting at him and bombs falling down around his head. A crying emotional woman in labor with his child made him feel absolutely useless. How was he supposed to help her? He wished he could take her pain and everything she was feeling. He would gladly bear it all to see her happy, he would do anything for her and his son.

To his relief Sheila finally pulled in front of the hospital where Claire worked and would now have the baby. Her mother was already waiting outside as they pulled up, along with another nurse with a wheelchair. Sheila and Daniel helped her out of the car just like they helped her in on the ride there.

When she was seated in the wheelchair her mom leaned over and gave her a squeeze. "I told you he was okay and you will be, too. We are all here for you."

"I know, Mom. I'm glad you're here," Claire replied, giving her mother a hug in return.

Esther turned to Daniel and threw her arms around him, planting a huge kiss on his cheek. "We were waiting for you to call, but showing up is better. Welcome to my family."

"Thanks, glad to be here." A blush crept up Daniel's cheeks this time. He felt a little overwhelmed with the acceptance he was receiving. Growing up alone he, was always pushed from home to home, never really making an emotional connection with anyone. With Claire he had a new family starting from a seedling. He had every intention to make sure it grew with strong roots.

Claire was wheeled into the hospital and to her private birthing room. Sheila let Daniel use the doctor's lounge to get cleaned up. Even though his uniform was dirty, he folded it neatly in his duffel bag and put on the scrubs that Sheila had given him. The only thing that remained of his uniform was his tan boots that he cleaned as best as he could before going into the room.

When he entered he saw Claire sitting up in a bed and crunching on ice chips. The monitor next to him charted out the beats of the baby's heart. As he walked over to take her hand, he thought there was no sound sweeter than the sound of his son's heartbeat in the room.

"How are you, my love?" he asked as he kissed her hand that he held.

"I'm four centimeters dilated and feeling no pain," she said with a bright smile.

Daniel looked over to Sheila, who was studying the monitor read out. "She opted for the meds."

Daniel nodded. "So it took the edge off the pain?"

Claire laughed. "Oh, babe, I am numb from the waist down."

"So what do we do now?"

"Well, Daniel, we wait until Danny decides he wants to grace us with his presence," Claire explained.

"So we are going to call him Danny?" Daniel's chest puffed out with pride.

"The way I see it, if I go around yelling Daniel for both of you, it could be a bit confusing."

Daniel's kiss said all that he needed to say. "I love you."

Claire caressed his face. "I love you, too."

"Hey hey! That's how she got into this mess, let's get his kid into the world before we begin work on another one!" Sheila joked.

"Um, I don't remember seeing you there when we worked on this one," Claire reminded her.

They were laughing when Esther walked back into the room with balloons. She asked what the joke was but no one answered. She shrugged and tied the balloons to a chair. The bright big balloons said, "Welcome" and "It's a Boy!" in sliver letters. It was only a matter of waiting until the baby made his entrance into the world.

* * * *

The hours were spent with Daniel and Claire catching up. Esther and Sheila were in the room sometimes, but quietly let the couple have their moments. Claire kept touching him to make sure he was real. She had worried so much about him, ached for him all those long months, and now to have him home were her prayers being answered. Every time a contraction made the monitor beep, he was there next to her. There was no pain, but the discomfort of tightening muscles in her belly was there as she contracted. Daniel rubbed her belly every time this happened, feeding her ice chips and asking so many questions that Sheila and the other nurses swore he was taking an exam on childbirth. He was being so sweet and so loving, Claire felt her eyes mist over just thinking about it. She thought she could have handled this part alone with just her mom and Sheila for support. Having him here with her proved she was wrong, she would have done it and ached for him every second of the time. She was a tough retired soldier, but when it came to love, she could be weak and know he would be there to catch her.

Finally after her final exam, the nurse told them she was fully dilated and ready to start pushing. The nurse put the call in to her doctor and started to prepare the bed for her delivery with Sheila's help.

"What are those for?' Daniel asked as Sheila pulled out the stirrups. When she explained Claire smiled as she saw Daniel turn visibly green.

"Uh, Daniel, you should be up here by my head," Claire said and moaned. Another contraction hit and this one she could feel. They had lowered the dosage on her epidural and now she could feel the pain of her labor once again.

Daniel moved frantically to her side with a wild look of panic on his face. "Why is she in pain, isn't she not supposed to be in pain!"

"We had to lower the dosage of the medication, Daniel, she needs to feel so she can push," Sheila said calmly.

"It's okay, Daniel," Claire said, holding out her hand to him. He grabbed it and she squeezed.

Everyone looked over to the door as it opened and Claire's doctor walked in. She was a tiny little woman who walked quickly into the room.

"Okay, Claire, I see you have a party here in this room." the doctor commented. "And who is this next to you? I didn't know we hired such handsome nurses."

Claire smiled. "Doctor Littleton, this is my soon to be husband, Sergeant Daniel Butler."

"Hmm, the Army is making them into some nice packages, aren't they?" Dr Littleton said as she sat on the stool between Claire's legs. "You're crowning, Claire, I can see some thick dark hair. I need for you to push for me like you mean it.

With Daniel behind her supporting her back, Claire tucked her chin into her chest and pushed. Words of encouragement filled the room and with every push Claire brought her son closer into the world. With one final low moan from Claire the cries of a new baby filled the air.

Daniel cut the cord that bound his son to the love of his life. He went back to Claire and kissed her reverently, their tears of joy mingling. Claire heard her mother sniffle softly in the background, and even Sheila looked on with tears in her eyes.

Claire looked on as Doctor Littleton handed Daniel his son. He sat next to Claire and stared at the new life in his arms.

"Thank you for this, for my son. Claire, you have made me the happiest man in the world. The only thing that is going to be better is when you become my wife," Daniel said.

"Baby, you couldn't get away from me if you tried," Claire replied softly. She touched the face of her new baby and whispered, "Happy birthday." She looked into the eyes of the man she loved. "Welcome home, Daniel, welcome home."

Epilogue

In a house next to the water in Washington, D.C., a new family lived. A dog barked in the backyard as Daniel Kirkland Butler aka "Danny," or "The Terror," took his first steps outside on the grass. Claire looked on with pride as Daniel encouraged his namesake to come to him. This soldier had found what he was searching for all his life. He'd found love and a family. Daniel had found a home.

About the Author

Dahlia Rose, bestselling author of contemporary erotica, suspense, and paranormal romance. She was born and raised on a Caribbean island and now currently lives in Charlotte, NC with her four kids whom she affectionately nicknamed "The children of the corn" and her biggest supporter/long time love. She has a love of erotica, dark fantasy, Sci-fi and the things that go bump in the night. Books and writing are her biggest passion and she hopes to open your imagination to the unknown between the pages of her books.

METROPOLITAN PASSION

these Urban Phaze titles
and more at phaze.com

9 781606 590683